Asha

The Princess of Matana

Written by Lenny Williams

Illustrated by Kaitlin Edwards

CreateSpace Independent Publishing

ISBN-10: 1546746331
ISBN-13: 978-1546746331

DEDICATION

After reading Jacqueline Jones' book 'Labor of Love, Labor of Sorrow' it informed me about the atrocities and torture that black women faced globally throughout the Atlantic slave trade era. During this time black women endured rape and other forms of brutal violence from the British, Spaniards, English Americans, Arabians, and more. I could honestly go on and on about how many groups of people abused black women on a global scale. It's really sad to say but during this time period black women's only freedom was either sleep or death. Often times they would tell their children and grandchildren folklores passed down from their ancestors. By telling these stories it would help take everyone's minds to a better place; this became a form of escapism from the plantation.

I can't imagine trying to cope through all of the situations my ancestors were put in especially the women. They witnessed their children being sold and taken away from them. They watched their husbands get severely beaten or killed for trying to protect them and use self-defense. And most of all they were repeatedly raped, and were viciously whipped if they resisted their rapist. Throughout all the horror black women continued to persevere, and uplifted black men while doing so. As a black man I've realized that black women have stood by our side even when we were at our weakest point. I would like to take this time out to thank every black woman out there who continues to fight for equality and justice. I really have no clue where we would be without you. When systematic racism and white supremacy had stripped black men from all forms of power, it did not know that one day it would have to face the wrath and power of our queens!

This book is dedicated to black women all over the world

CONTENTS

lennysimagination.com

ACKNOWLEDGMENTS

I want to thank my illustrator, Kaitlin Edwards, for bringing my vision to life. For a year and a half you worked extremely hard to provide the best illustrations an author could ask for! I'm definitely looking forward to working with you again.

To my readers: As you read this fairytale you will notice that I've created a country in Africa called Matana. The royal people in this country will be wearing red, black, and green stripes on their uniforms. I had their uniforms designed that way to represent the Black Liberation Flag. According to The Universal Negro Improvement Association, Red = the blood that unites all people of Black African ancestry, and shed for liberation. Black = black people whose existence as a nation, though not a nation-state, is affirmed by the existence of the flag. Green = the abundant natural wealth of Africa.

Thank you all for continuing to support my dreams, and as always I hope that you enjoy reading this book as much as I enjoyed writing it.

ASHA

The Princess of Matana

CHAPTER ONE

LEAVING THE CITY

As the evening darkened, a young man named Jamal and his best friend Tamir took pictures of the night sky. They were on the rooftop of their condominium, trying to capture a magical photograph to enter in an art contest they'd heard about on the radio. Winning this contest would earn them $100,000 and a free trip to Africa.

Jamal was more concerned about life after college than winning the contest, though. While they were taking shots of the stars, Jamal looked over at his friend and asked, "What do you plan on doing after we graduate this year?"

Tamir put down his camera and began to think. "I don't know, man," he finally answered. "To be honest, I just want to continue what we've been doing. If you think about it, we've pretty much accomplished all of our goals. Our photography business, T and J's Photos, is doing extremely well, and we also have a decent amount of money all to ourselves."

Jamal scratched his head and smiled. "Yeah, you're right, bro—but for some reason, I'm not satisfied with just

being here in the city. Maybe that's why I love taking pictures of the sky so much: it constantly changes. It reminds me that there's more to life than just this city."
Tamir laughed. "Man, why do you always have to get so deep? It sounds like you just need a vacation, that's all. Besides, if we win this contest, we'll get a free trip out of the city and $100,000 in our pockets."

The next morning, when Jamal was getting dressed for school, he looked in the mirror and began to talk to himself. "All right, all you have to do is pass your Marketing and Photography finals, and then you're completely finished with college," he said. "After that, you just have to be ready for whatever happens next in your life."
When he headed downstairs, he could smell his mother

(Mrs. Howard) cooking turkey bacon and his father (Mr. Howard) making pancakes. "Good morning, baby! Are you hungry?" Mrs. Howard asked as she hugged him.

"Yes, I am!" Jamal replied as he rubbed his hands together and inhaled the smell of breakfast.

"Good morning, you soon-to-be graduate!" Mr. Howard said while patting his son on the back.

"Good morning, Dad," Jamal answered with a grin.

"Have you and Tamir figured out if you're going to throw a party or something after graduation?" Mr. Howard wondered.

That made Jamal start to think about the night before. "Nah, we're pretty much just focused on winning this art contest," he explained. "That's all."

Mrs. Howard was shocked by this revelation. "What! You don't want a graduation party? But Mrs. Sanders and I have been preparing you and Tamir's party for years!"

Jamal started giggling. "Mom, it's just a graduation!" he protested. "I don't need a party."

"It's your college graduation! I've thrown a party for all of your other graduations, and I won't miss out on planning your last one," she insisted.

At that point, Jamal's little sister Maya intervened in their conversation. "You better listen to Momma," she warned.

Shrugging, Jamal smiled. "All right, Mom, you win: I'll have the party."

Moments later, they were all plopped on the couch in front of the TV. Jamal was on his third plate of pancakes, Mrs. Howard was fixing up Maya's hair before she went off to school, and Mr. Howard was reading the newspaper. For some odd reason, Mrs. Howard could sense that something was bothering Jamal. "What's wrong, Jamal?" she wondered.

Jamal turned to his mother with a confused look on his face. "Oh, nothing, Mom... Why?"
Mrs. Howard wasn't buying it. "Because I have a mother's intuition. You seem a little down, honey, that's all."

"Mom, he probably needs a girlfriend," Maya interjected with a giggle.

"Now, Maya, that wasn't nice," Mrs. Howard chastised while still combing her daughter's hair. "But you know," she mused, "she might be right."

Jamal shook his head in embarrassment. "Oh God, you guys, I'm fine!" he said.

Mr. Howard had put down his newspaper and started listening to their conversation. He was beginning to sense that something was wrong with Jamal as well. "No, I can tell something is bothering you, son," he said seriously. "What's wrong?"

Jamal sighed and finally gave in. "All right, I guess I'm just not satisfied with everything I've done in my life so far. I just want to get out of the city and travel somewhere far away."

"Like a road trip or something?" Maya asked.

"Yeah, exactly. I want to go to places I've never been before and experience different cultures," Jamal explained.

"Wow, that's fascinating, Jamal! Listen—you're a great person and a well-accomplished young man. You can do whatever you put your mind to," Mrs. Howard offered with a wide smile.

As Jamal was starting to leave, his father stopped him to give him some advice. "Hey, your mother's right," he said. "You're an incredible young man, and you've made us all so proud. You own a business, and you're about to graduate college. So whatever your heart is telling you to do, just go for it."

"Thanks, Dad! I sure will," Jamal answered him as they hugged each other.

"Love ya, son."

"Love ya too, Dad."

As Jamal was on his way out the door, Mrs. Howard came running toward him. "HEY JAMAL!" she shouted. Jamal instantly stopped in his tracks and turned around with a displeased look on his face. "Yes, Mom?" he replied.

"The Sanders are dropping Maya off at school today, so can you take her upstairs with you?"

Jamal gritted his teeth and smiled. "Sure, no problem, Mom," he said.

Jamal and Maya then headed upstairs to the Sanders' condo to meet up with Tamir and his little sister Aaliyah.

After hearing the doorbell ring, Mr. Sanders placed his big empty cereal bowl on the ground and ran to the door. "Hey, Jamal and Maya! How are you?" he asked after opening it.

"We're doing good, Mr. Sanders. My mom and dad said thanks for taking Maya to school," Jamal answered as he and Maya walked in the door.

Mrs. Sanders had just finished picking out Aaliyah's hair. "Does it look like yours, Mommy?" Aaliyah was asking as she felt her hairdo.

"Yes, baby, it looks just like mine," Mrs. Sanders confirmed.

"Yay!" Aaliyah shouted with joy.

Rising to her feet, Mrs. Sanders pulled out waffles, eggs, and sausages from the warmer. "So are you two hungry?" she asked Jamal and Maya.

"Yes, ma'am," Jamal said while staring at the food and rubbing his hands.

Maya gave Jamal a shocked look. "But Jamal, we just ate," she whispered.

"Well, you know me: I can't resist waffles," Jamal

whispered back.

When Aaliyah spotted Maya, she quickly ran toward her. "Hey, did you bring Brownie?" she asked.

"Yup, here he is," Maya said as she pulled out her pet hamster from her backpack.

Aaliyah started to jump up and down, clapping. "Yay! I have Sunshine upstairs in her cage. I know she wants to see him. Come on!" she said as they ran upstairs to her room.

In the living room, Jamal noticed that Tamir was sitting on the couch, completely focused on his phone. "What's up, bro?" he asked. "Is everything all right? It's not like you to pass up on food."

Tamir quickly glanced up from his phone to answer Jamal. "I know, man—I've just been studying all morning. I don't think I'm prepared for this Marketing final at all. I know I'm going to ace the Photography final because that's easy, but this Marketing final may hurt my GPA," he explained.

Jamal grabbed Tamir's keys off the key hanger and stuffed his face with one more waffle. "Don't worry about a thing, man. Look, I'll drive us to school so you can have more time to study."

Tamir took a deep breath in relief. "Thanks, bro. I really needed this. I should've studied harder this week, but I've just been focused on winning the $100,000."

During their drive to school, Tamir brought up the art contest again. "Man, we really have a shot at winning this contest," he said while still looking at the study materials on his phone.

Jamal felt more skeptical about the whole thing. "I honestly have doubts because we're dealing with so much competition. There are digital artists, painters, photographers, and graphic designers entered in this contest, and we have to stand out from all of them."

Tamir continued to disagree, however. "Nope, I have a

feeling we are still going to win this with ease," he said. "It's destined to happen. Think about it: you're always talking about getting out of the city and traveling far away. This is exactly what you need!"

"All right, I'm with you bro: we are going to win the $100,000 and that trip to Africa," Jamal answered with enthusiasm.

"That's what I'm talking about! What country in Africa did they pick for the prize winners to visit?" Tamir queried.

"I believe it's called Matana," Jamal replied.

"Oh yeah." Tamir grinned. "They have some beautiful women over there."

Jamal shook his head. "That's true!" he agreed.

CHAPTER TWO

ROYAL TRADITIONS

Meanwhile, in the magical country of Matana, Africa, a young princess named Asha was growing tired and frustrated of practicing the kingdom's royal traditions.

Her father (King Juma) and mother (Queen Naomi) were trying to convince her that she needed to accept the arranged marriage they'd planned for her. "Sweetheart, this is a tradition that our ancestors have been practicing for thousands of years. Can you at least try to understand that? If you don't agree to the marriage, the curse of Zimmer and Zelda will destroy our kingdom," King Juma frantically explained.

Asha took a very deep breath to relieve her stress. "Dad, this kingdom is not cursed! Nothing bad ever happens here!" she exclaimed.

King Juma placed his hands on his forehead and shook his head side to side. "That's because everyone has abided by our ancestors' royal rules. The curse cannot affect us if we don't allow it to enter our lives."

Queen Naomi stepped down from her throne to talk to Asha as well. "You are our only child and the next heir to the throne, Asha," she said gently. "You have to understand that this is your destiny."

Asha frowned and folded her arms over her chest. "I just want to meet a man who's had different experiences than me. I believe I want someone who has lived outside of Matana."

King Juma and Queen Naomi both sighed. "We'll talk about this later," King Juma said.

That evening, Asha stepped outside the walls of the palace and sat near the front gates to relax. She was soon joined by her best friend Halima and their pet lion cub, Azi. Noticing that Asha had a gloomy look on her face, Halima asked, "What's wrong?"

"I've just been thinking a lot lately," Asha replied grumpily. "Like, what's the point of an arranged marriage? You never have an actual chance of choosing the love of your life because your parents do it for you."

"I guess that's true, but I always thought it was best not to ask those type of questions," Halima answered.

"Why?" Asha wondered.

"You know, because maybe our parents are just looking out for us. They have to know what's best for us… Right?" Halima replied.

"No! It's just a stupid tradition of royal people marrying other royal people," Asha told her.

"Well, where do you expect to find the man of your

dreams, anyway?" Halima asked sarcastically.

Asha sighed. "Ugh... I don't know. He's probably out there somewhere," she responded glumly.

Turning away, Halima whistled to Azi to get his attention. "Azi, come here, boy! Come here!" she called.

Azi jumped onto Halima's lap and licked her face. "Hey, Azi boy," she said with a smile. "Here, take this note and give it to Namdi, okay?" she told him as she attached a note to his collar.

Leaning toward Azi to feed him a mango, Asha began to pet him. "Aw, poor Azi. I know you don't want to spend your day running errands for Halima—do you, boy?" she cooed.

Halima giggled. "Oh geez, he's just doing me a favor. And besides, Azi loves to run around the kingdom all day. I'm just putting his energy to good use."

Asha gave Halima a mysterious look. "I see... So you're sending notes to Namdi now, huh?"

Halima gently scratched her forehead and thought about what to say. "Not exactly; he actually sent me a note, and I'm just replying to it," she finally answered.

"What did he say?" Asha wondered.

"He just wanted to know if I wanted to hang out with him tonight at the graduation party."

"And what did you say?" Asha asked as she folded her arms.

Halima wiped her forehead in embarrassment. "Um...I said yes."

Asha exhaled heavily through her nose. "HALIMA! You promised me that we both wouldn't date these royal guys!"

Halima placed both of her hands over her face to hide her shame. "They aren't so bad once you get to know them!" she told Asha.

"THEY AREN'T SO BAD? They're arrogant, demanding, and believe that they're the best-looking men on the planet," Asha retorted passionately.

"Oh please, Asha, just give it a shot! And besides, Namdi is cute," Halima answered as she removed her hands from her face.

Asha sucked her teeth. "You're basically giving into our parents' wishes. Your parents love Namdi; they've probably already planned an arranged marriage for you two. You do know that, right?"

Halima was becoming irritated with Asha's rant. "Asha, your parents are already planning a marriage between you and Yoba, with or without your consent. Do you know that? Since your parents think Yoba is such a great guy, maybe you should give him a chance."

"My parents only love Yoba because he has the same name as my ancestor. They believe it's some big coincidence, but I know his family named him Yoba on purpose so that he could one day become king. And Yoba is a big flirt anyway; he's always telling girls—especially the tourists—to touch his dreads and his muscles," Asha explained angrily.

Halima had grown tired of arguing and just wanted to have fun. "Look, I'm going to hang out with Namdi at the party tonight. Not only will Yoba be there, but so will all of our classmates. You know that they would all love to see you. You're the princess of Matana and the most popular girl around—so just come and enjoy the night, Asha."

Asha gave Halima a nonchalant look. "No, that's okay, I'm good. I'm just going to go to bed. I'll see you tomorrow," she said.

"Okay," Halima replied as they hugged each other and said their goodbyes.

Later that night at the graduation party, Halima was hanging out with Namdi, Yoba, and the rest of their college friends. "Hey Halima, where's Asha?" Yoba asked.

"She's not feeling so well. You'll probably see her tomorrow," Halima explained.

"Aw, I was looking forward to seeing her. You don't think you can convince her to come out?" Yoba wondered.

"No, sorry. She's really not feeling well today," Halima told him sympathetically.

"Oh Yoba, leave the poor girl alone! You'll have plenty of time to nag your future queen once you get married." Namdi said as he put his arms around Halima and walked away with her.

"So who do you think our future son is going to look like, me or you?" Namdi asked Halima once they were alone, awkwardly trying to flirt.

Halima looked disgusted after she heard that. "WHAT?" she shouted.

"What's wrong?" Namdi wondered in confusion.

"Really, the first thing you ask me is what I think our son will look like?" She glared at him.

"Well, what am I supposed to say?" Namdi asked, still bewildered.

"What about 'HEY, HOW WAS YOUR DAY?' or 'HEY, HOW HAVE YOU BEEN?'" Halima demanded.

"Geez, Halima, relax! We can talk about all that stuff after you're my wife. Right now, I'm thinking about the future of our children," Namdi explained as he tried to take her hands.

Halima instantly yanked her hands away from him. "You guys are truly idiots," she informed Namdi as she stormed off.

THE PRINCESS OF MATANA

That night before going to bed, Asha washed her face and gazed at the stars for a while. "Dear ancestors, please help my parents understand me as I continue to grow, and please help me find my future king," she whispered.

She then heard a knock at the door. "Who is it?" she asked.

"It's me, Halima. Can I come in?"

"Sure," Asha replied.

Halima walked into Asha's room with a sad face. "Is the party over already?" Asha wondered.

"No... Namdi just got on my nerves, so I left," Halima explained. Thinking about their conversation from earlier that day, she then hopped onto Asha's couch. "Hey Asha, what's the point of an arranged marriage?" she drawled mockingly.

After Halima's question, they both began to laugh hysterically.

CHAPTER THREE

THE FACE

After completing their final exams, Jamal and Tamir rushed to look for places in the city to take pictures.

"Hey, do you think you passed your marketing final?" Jamal asked.

Tamir was nonchalant. "I think I did pretty good. I don't know why I was so worried. Anyway, now that we've got that out the way we can focus on this contest."

Jamal suddenly noticed that the fiery disk of the sun seemed to be melting and shimmering into the shape of a human face. He shoved Tamir. "Yo Tamir, look at that!" He pointed. The face became more distinct: it was that of a beautiful woman.

"Whoa! Is that—is that a face in the sky?" Tamir grabbed his camera.

Jamal also began snapping pictures of the countenance. "We've gotta get a better angle and see this thing closer up," he said.

"Okay, yeah, good idea, but uh...how do we do that?" Tamir's glance jerked around at the stream of people walking blithely past them, oblivious to the sky. "And how come nobody else is seeing what we're seeing??"

"I don't know! But we have to get on top of a building! ASAP!"

Jamal and Tamir lurched through the crowd and into the tallest building they could find. Fortunately the elevator was free. After they had reached the rooftop, Tamir setup a tripod and Jamal placed his camera on it and began steadily taking pictures of the mystery woman's exotic countenance, doing his best to suppress his excitement for the sake of the job but transfixed by her beauty. Beautiful brown skin, fine ropelike locks of hair, and my God what luscious lips. Who was she?

Suddenly the face vanished.

"Any good shots?" Tamir squealed.

Jamal checked his camera, clicking through the images of the pictures he had taken. "Come on. Come on. Come on. Darn, most of these pics came out blurry. Wait...okay, yeah, hold on, yeah, all right, we got one!!"

Tamir clenched his fist in excitement. "Great! We've got this contest in the bag now. But, man, talk about freaky. How in the world did this happen? It was like magic or something."

Jamal nodded gravely. "Yeah. That's exactly what it was. Magic!"

When Jamal and Tamir visited the City Art Institute to submit a print of the photograph to the contest, one of the judges who happened to be there at the time seemed a bit stunned. "Wow! This is a very good edit!"

"We didn't edit this picture, sir," Jamal said.

"Yeah, the face was really there," Tamir chimed in. But they were worried. Would their submission be disqualified on the basis of some alleged Photoshopping?

The judge gave them a look. "Uh huh. Well, you know it doesn't matter whether this was edited or not. It's still art. Very imaginative. Very striking. In fact, this may be the best thing we've seen all week."

Jamal smiled. "Really!?"

The man nodded. "We'll be making a decision very soon. If you win you'll receive a call. Probably tomorrow."

"Great!" said Tamir.

"Well, you know, don't count your chickens. You've got a lot of competition," the judge said. But he winked.

Two days later Jamal received a call. It was the news he'd hoped for. He and Tamir had won the art contest.

He rushed to see Tamir. "You were right, bro! We did it! We won!"

"Yeah, well, I told you it was destined to happen, man! Matana here we come!"

They gathered their families together to tell them the news.

"Mom…Dad, we won!" Tamir told his parents.

"That's right, our photograph got the top prize," Jamal told his parents. "We won the $100,000 and a free trip to Matana, Africa."

Their families were extremely proud and excited for them. Mrs. Howard gave them a hug. "Congratulations, guys! I'm so proud of you."

"Our babies are going to be superstars!" Mrs. Sanders said as she got her hugs in next.

Mr. Howard was more down to earth. "So let's see this triumphant photograph."

Jamal presented a print of the photo of the face of the woman in the sky. "Here it is, Dad."

Mr. Sanders inspected it also. "The editing on this.... Wow. You two have great editing skills. I can see how much thought and effort you put into this. For a second I thought that woman's face was really in the clouds. No seam or any telltale sign at all, so far as I can tell. Yes. Good work. Really good work."

Their parents seemed genuinely impressed by the photograph. But the boys were innocent of the artifice being attributed to them and the praise made them a little uncomfortable.

Jamal gave Tamir a look. If only we could tell them, the look said. But they both knew that they had to keep what had happened—whatever exactly that might have been—to themselves for now.

"Thanks, Dad," Tamir said. "It was, uh, you know, hard work, but we did what we could."

Looking at the picture he had taken with fresh eyes, Jamal became even more curious about who the beautiful woman could possibly be.

"Do you think she's a ghost?" he asked Tamir when they were alone again. "Or an angel maybe?"

Tamir shrugged. "I'm as clueless as you are, man. I know one thing though. This was a sign. You better believe it. This was a true sign."

A few evenings later, the City Art Institute threw a party for Jamal and Tamir. A family photo was taken as they flourished the $100,000 check they had earned.

"Hey don't forget to bring me something back, big head," Aaliyah told Tamir.

Maya ran to Jamal and hugged him tight as she could. "You won't be gone for too long, will you, big bro?"
Jamal shook his head. "Nah. I'll just be gone for three days that's all. Three days. We'll be back just in time for my graduation. You're gonna be there right?"
"Definitely!"

CHAPTER FOUR

FALLING HARD

After Jamal and Tamir's flight landed in Matana, their tour guide met them at the front of the airport. "Hello, guys!" the man exclaimed. "I'm guessing you two are the famous photographers everyone's talking about?"
Tamir snickered and shrugged. "I guess so," he replied.
"All right. Well, come along. My name is Mr. Kwame, by the way, and I will be your guide for the entire day."
While checking into the Matana Resort, Jamal and Tamir noticed their photograph of the mystery woman hanging up in the lobby. "Oh, so I see that you're looking at the picture you took," Mr. Kwame said as he joined the guys in staring at it. "I'm guessing you found a photo of the princess on the Internet and edited your picture of the sky with it?"
Jamal could no longer hold his tongue. "No, sir, this picture is real. We didn't edit a thing."
Mr. Kwame began to laugh hysterically at that, saying, "Okay, you're pulling my leg!"
"Just forget it, man," Tamir said. Leaning closer to Jamal,

he whispered, "It's going to be hard to convince people that we saw the sun turn into a woman's face."

"Yeah, I guess you're right," Jamal whispered back. "And did he just say that she was a princess?"

When Tamir didn't answer, Jamal tapped Mr. Kwame's shoulder. "Excuse me, uh, Mr. Kwame, did you just say that the woman in our picture is a princess?"

"Yes, she is the princess of Matana. Are you telling me you two didn't know that?" Mr. Kwame asked incredulously.

"No," Tamir answered.

Mr. Kwame started laughing again. "Okay, now you're really pulling my leg!"

After checking into the resort, the first place Mr. Kwame took them was the safari. As they both took pictures of the wild animals roaming around freely, Tamir began to feel a little frightened. "This is kind of scary, man. What if this truck just runs out of gas? What are we going to do then?" he demanded.

"Let's just hope that doesn't happen," Jamal replied. "I'm pretty sure they filled the tank before we took off."

"All right, let me just take my mind off of thinking negatively. Are you getting any good pictures?" Tamir wondered.

"Yeah—look at this shot I took of the giraffes. I know my mom is going to love this picture," Jamal answered as he let Tamir have a look at his camera.

Suddenly, the truck stopped by a narrow river surrounded by tall grass. "What's going on?" Tamir asked while putting his camera down.

"I have no clue," Jamal replied.

Mr. Kwame hopped out of the truck and walked up to a bulky kayak that was bobbing in the water. "All right, guys, your journey does not end here; it only continues. This is the Matana River, and we will be taking this three-person kayak upstream," he explained.

Hearing that, Tamir looked extremely timid. "Okay, so nothing will jump out of the grass or the water and kill us, right?" he asked nervously.

Mr. Kwame chuckled. "Loosen up, young man. You'll be fine. Trust me, everything is peaceful around here. And our wildlife workers are the best at what they do, so I can assure you that you'll be fine."

"Tamir, calm down. I'm sure he wouldn't be our tour guide if he didn't know what he was doing," Jamal told Tamir as he tried to get him to relax.

"Okay, I'm all good—but if I die, I want my tombstone to say, 'Here lies Tamir. It was all Jamal's and Mr. Kwame's fault.' Got that?" Tamir demanded.

After they boarded the kayak, Mr. Kwame paddled them up the river, while Jamal and Tamir continued to take pictures of anything that caught their attention. While looking around, Jamal spotted a waterfall up ahead. "Hey, Mr. Kwame, should we turn around!" he yelled.

"Yeah, I'm not to trying to fall to my death here,"

Tamir added fearfully.

"It's okay, guys! This is the best part. There is actually a big boulder near the edge of the waterfall which will prevent us from falling over it," Mr. Kwame explained.

"I hope you're right about this!" Tamir said as they got closer and closer to the edge of the waterfall.

"I'm with Tamir on that!" Jamal agreed anxiously.

When they hit the big boulder, though, the kayak stopped, just as Mr. Kwame had predicted. "THANK GOD WE'RE STILL ALIVE!" Tamir shouted in celebration while holding his hand over his heart.

Mr. Kwame then pointed at something way across the river. "Now, look way over there," he advised.

When Jamal and Tamir looked across the river, they were astonished by what they saw. The place looked like an ancient civilization. There was a huge wall with gigantic statues on each end. Behind the wall, they could see a glimpse of some huge buildings and enormous mountains. They could also see two guards standing in front of the entrance to this place.

"Whoa, what is that? Is that another city or something?" Jamal asked.

"Nope, that is Matana Kingdom," Mr. Kwame told them cheerfully.

"Wow, an actual kingdom! Are there any more kingdoms around here?" Jamal asked as he became more curious.

"I'm afraid not; this is the only one left. There used to be plenty of kingdoms on this continent many years ago, but invaders destroyed them. They couldn't destroy Matana Kingdom, though, because this is the most sacred one. This kingdom is so sacred that even the animals protect it from intruders," Mr. Kwame informed them.

"Oh, okay—so do the people that live over there train the animals?" Tamir asked.

"No, the animals already know how to protect the kingdom without being trained. It's a sacred place, remember. Oh yeah, and the woman from your picture, the princess...she lives over there as well." Mr. Kwame smiled.

Jamal instantly became excited. "Really! She does? Can you take us there? I would love to meet her. I could show her our picture," he said.

While Jamal was speaking, however, all Mr. Kwame could do was shake his head from side to side. "Sorry, I can't do that: it's forbidden," he answered. "Only royal people and the animals that protect the kingdom can go in and out as they please. I wish there was more I could do, but, unfortunately, I can't. We just have to continue moving along with the tour."

Mr. Kwame was about to start paddling again, but Jamal stopped him. "Wait, uh, one more thing. Will the princess ever come out to the resort or to any of the non-royal places around here?"

Mr. Kwame rubbed his chin as he thought about it. "You know, it's actually very rare for the king, the queen, or the princess to leave the kingdom. And when they do, it's usually for a big event. Like, a few days ago, the princess and the rest of her graduating class from the kingdom had their graduation ceremony here at the resort in the auditorium. It was a big fiasco, too. Everyone was lined up to catch a glimpse of the king and queen as they watched their daughter walk across the stage to receive her degree. But, like I was saying, whenever they do come up here with us regular citizens, it's a huge parade."

Jamal's expression had changed from excited to unenthusiastic. "Oh, okay—I see," he answered sadly.

Mr. Kwame felt kind of guilty for making Jamal lose hope in meeting the princess, so he decided to help him regain some hope again. "Hey, I'm certain something will come up during the weekend. If I see her stop by the resort, I'll be sure to let you know, okay?" he offered.

After guiding Jamal and Tamir around Matana throughout the rest of the day, Mr. Kwame gave them a brochure that consisted of things they could do during the rest of their trip. As they relaxed in their room at the resort that evening, Tamir read through the brochure and talked about all of their fun options for activities. "Yo!" he exclaimed at one point while pacing the room in excitement. "Look at this: they have a mall with an amusement park and water park inside. We have to go there tomorrow!"

"Sounds great," Jamal replied. He was sitting down and looking through the pictures on his camera. "Ugh!" he added, "Every picture I took of the kingdom came out blurry because the kayak kept rocking. Did you take any shots of it?"

"Nah, I forgot to—but it's probably a good thing we didn't. You heard what Mr. Kwame said: that place is cursed! Our cameras would've probably shattered if we took pictures of it," Tamir joked.

Jamal laughed. "Mr. Kwame said it was sacred, not cursed," he answered. "But I really need to get this picture, man."

Tamir sighed and fell backwards onto the couch. "Jamal, I love taking pictures just as much as you do, but can't we take a break this weekend and have some fun? I'm trying to meet some Matana girls and enjoy myself!"

Jamal finally put his camera down and took a look at the brochure. "Okay, you're right. I'm trying to enjoy myself, too, but I have to get this picture first thing tomorrow morning. Bro, I swear this will be the last time we take pictures while we're here," he promised.

"All right. Well, I'm definitely going to get a good sleep, then," Tamir replied tiredly.

The next morning, they walked around outside of the resort to find the Matana River. "We have to be able to find that river somewhere around here without going through the safari again," Jamal had said.

Tamir suddenly began to check his pockets. "Let's check the brochure! I have it right here." Finally finding the brochure, he pulled it out. "It says here that we'll see the Matana River if we walk two miles along the Matana nature trail."

After spotting the river two miles into the trail, Jamal grabbed one of the kayaks that were lined up near the riverbank. "Dang! The sign says these are for staff use only," he said.

Tamir looked around to see if anyone was near them. "Well, no one is around. We could probably get away with borrowing it," he answered as they hopped onto the kayak and started to paddle upstream.

As Jamal and Tamir got close to the waterfall moments later, they became worried. "I don't think we should go through with this," Tamir mentioned.

"Yeah, I'm getting a bad feeling, too," Jamal agreed. "Let's turn around."

Right after Jamal spoke, though, a water current pushed them directly into the boulder at the edge of the

falls. "Woah!" Tamir shouted as he took deep breaths.
"It's all right, we're all good; all I have to do is get a good picture of the kingdom, and then we're out of here," Jamal answered, trying to keep calm as he stood up in the kayak to take better pictures.

"Okay, cool—how are they coming out?" Tamir asked while making sure that the coast was still clear and the boat was steady.

"They're decent, but I wish there was a way I could get closer," Jamal answered.

"I've got an idea!" Tamir offered. "If I'm able to scoot the kayak up just a tad bit, then you will be able to take the perfect picture—but I'm going to need your help."

"All right." Jamal placed his camera around his neck and sat back down in the kayak, adding, "Okay, let's scoot it on the count of three. One...two...three!"

Right after they counted to three, however, the boulder that was supporting them suddenly moved, and the kayak fell straight down the waterfall. The fall led them crashing into a bigger river with a stronger current, the flow of the rushing water swept them closer and closer to Matana Kingdom.

While swimming against the current, Jamal spotted the kayak right behind him. "The kayak is still intact—grab on to it!" he shouted.

Just as he and Tamir hopped onto the kayak, though, a huge shark poked its head above shore and bit the kayak in half. "OH NO!" Tamir shouted as he and Jamal fell back into the river again.

Luckily, the current pushed them onto land shortly after the shark attack. They were now about a mile across from the kingdom.

"I didn't think we were going to make it out of that river alive," Jamal gasped, breathing heavily.

"Word, man. Let's get out of here!" Tamir replied.

As they started walking along the shoreline they

couldn't help but stop and stare at the kingdom again. "This place looks surreal," Jamal murmured to his friend. "Now that we're closer, let me take a—wait, where's my camera?" Jamal began to frantically search all around himself, and Tamir quickly noticed that he didn't have his camera either. "I lost mine too, man!" he shouted. "This sucks: first we get soaked, then attacked by a shark, and now we've lost our cameras."

CHAPTER FIVE

THE ENCOUNTER

While Asha and Halima were outside playing with their lion cub Azi and his parents Afia and Asad, they suddenly heard footsteps near the shore. Asad ran straight through the jungle toward the riverbank, roaring loudly to get the attention of the rest of the animals that protected the kingdom.

Jamal and Tamir stopped in their tracks. "Wait—what's that noise, and why is the ground shaking?" Jamal gasped. After hearing another deafening roar, Tamir turned slowly toward Jamal and answered, "The animals!"

They tried to run back to the river, but there were still too many sharks swimming in it. Left with no other options, they decided to hide in an area with high grass.

Despite their efforts to hide, though, Asad instantly picked up their smell. He immediately plowed through the grass and knocked both of them onto their backs. As Asad stood over Jamal and Tamir with a paw on each of their chests, the rest of the animals surrounded the perimeter so that they couldn't escape.

A few minutes later, Asha and Halima came running through the grass, holding their spears. "Who are you two?" Asha demanded.

Jamal and Tamir could not see who was speaking to them because Asad was still growling in their faces. "I'm Jamal," Jamal answered bravely.

"And I'm Tamir," Tamir added.

Halima threw her spear into the ground with force. "No, you're trespassers—that's what you are!" she cried.

"No, not at all!" Jamal protested. "I can explain everything if you give me a chance!"

"And if you could keep this lion from eating us, that would be great," Tamir put in.

Halima began to pet Asad. "All right," she murmured, "at ease, Asad. At ease." She guided the lion away from the guys. "Okay, explain yourselves!"

As Jamal and Tamir stood up they saw Asha's face and became speechless. "She looks just like the woman I saw in the sky! She has the same beautiful brown skin, the same fine, rope-like locks of hair, and those were her lips, all right—looking luscious and irresistible," Jamal thought to himself.

"Well, are you going to talk or not?" Asha demanded.

Jamal snapped out of his daze. "You're the woman in the sky; I mean, the woman from the sky," he said.

Asha was very confused and did not know what Jamal was talking about. "What?" she asked.

Jamal smiled. "You're princess Asha, right?"

Asha nodded. "Yes, I am."

"Okay. Well, Princess Asha, my friend and I saw your face in the sky," Jamal explained.

Tamir intervened to help back up Jamal's story. "Yes, he's right: we saw the sun turn into your face."

Asha and Halima didn't believe a word they were saying. "Nice try, but we aren't falling for this crazy act," Halima told them.

"Now, how did you get here?" Asha demanded.

"Well, I was taking pictures of your kingdom at the top of the waterfall over there, but we fell off and landed in the river and got washed up on shore," Jamal offered.

Asha smirked. "Oh, okay then. You see, isn't it easier when you tell the truth?"

"We never lied to you," Tamir denied.

"Whatever," Halima replied as she rolled her eyes.

"So, where are you from?" Asha asked, looking between the two boys.

"We're from America, but we won a free weekend trip here. We're staying up at the resort," Jamal explained.

"What part of America are you from?" Halima wondered.

"We're from the City," Tamir answered.

"All right, now that we've established everything, I will have someone send you back to the resort," Asha declared authoritatively.

"Yes!" Tamir shouted in excitement.

Jamal, however, was shaking his head. "Hold on.

Uh...can we see what the kingdom looks like inside?" he asked.

"No way—it's forbidden!" Halima said.

Jamal walked toward Asha and gently took one of her hands. Looking into her eyes as she looked into his, he said, "Please, Asha—I've always wanted to travel the world to see what life was like outside of the City. This kingdom looks wonderful, and I know it's sacred, so I would never do anything to harm or destroy it. I just want to experience what life is like here."

Giving in, Asha smiled. "Well, okay, but we're going to have to sneak you guys in," she agreed. "The guards and people here are really strict about letting in outsiders."

Halima tapped Asha's arm. "Um, can I speak to you for a moment?" she whispered.

Asha nodded and took her friend aside. "What's wrong?" she asked.

"Are you sure we can trust them? This seems really dangerous. What if they reveal the secrets of our kingdom to the entire world?" Halima wondered.

"They won't. I know we can trust them," Asha replied confidently.

"How do you know that?" Halima asked.

"When I looked into Jamal's eyes, I could tell he was being honest, and I believe he's trustworthy," Asha explained.

"But they're probably crazy! You heard what they said, right? They think they saw your face in the sky!" Halima exclaimed.

"Well, what if they really did? I think we should just give them a chance," Asha insisted.

"Okay, but I'm hoping you weren't just bit by the love bug," Halima told her while giggling.

"No way!" Asha responded as she waved Halima off.

While Asha and Halima were talking, Jamal and Tamir were having their own conversation. "Listen, man—I don't think this is a good idea. Let's just go back to the resort," Tamir was saying.

"Aw, come on. This might be fun! We should give it a try," Jamal answered with a grin.

"Do you see the statues over there? They look like giants that are about to come to life! I don't know, bro—something about this place just gives me the creeps," Tamir replied with a shudder.

Jamal laughed and patted his friend on the back. "That's because you're a city guy, but we'll get adjusted to this place in no time."

"Ugh…if you say so!" Tamir answered uncertainly. Asha then whistled to her elephant for a ride. "Dayo, come here, boy!" she yelled.

As Dayo came trotting toward Asha and Halima, the ground began to tremble. "Woah, that thing is gigantic!" Tamir said in awe.

"He's not a thing—he's an elephant, silly," Halima corrected.

"All right, all right, I'm sorry. And are you two sure we won't get caught?" Tamir asked the girls.

"No, you won't get caught; luckily, we know our way around the entire kingdom," Halima answered as she took Tamir by the hand to help him climb on top of Dayo. Asha followed suit, helping Jamal climb up. She then had one of her gorillas fetch a basket.

"Here, you two: lay down in the basket. We're going to hide you in here until we get to Asha's palace," Halima explained.

As Asha and Halima entered the kingdom, Jamal and Tamir peeked through the tiny holes in the basket atop the elephant to see what was going on. They saw a bunch of royal people walking around dressed exactly like Asha and Halima, wearing white silk shirts with red, black, and green stripes on them. The guards carried staffs and wore white silk shirts with blue and gold garments. The boys also noticed that there was gold everywhere: on the walls, the steps, the doors... Even the people were wearing gold. "Man, everything in here must be worth trillions," Tamir whispered to Jamal.

"Shush!" Halima said as she slapped the basket to keep them quiet. "So where are we going to put them in your palace?" she then whispered to Asha.

"They can stay in the attic in my room. No one ever goes up there," Asha whispered back.

After Dayo took them to Asha's front door, Halima had

Jamal and Tamir quickly hop out of the basket and run inside. "Hurry! Follow me straight to the attic," Halima said as she pulled down the ladder from the ceiling.

Jamal and Tamir climbed up the ladder and gasped as they entered the attic. "All I can say is, wow!" Jamal said as he looked around.

Tamir sprinted toward one of the windows and said, "You can see the entire kingdom from this view."

"And from what I saw downstairs, your room looks more like a house!" Jamal told Asha.

Halima and Asha couldn't believe that these two guys thought that everything they laid their eyes on was amazing. "Why are you two so impressed by my attic?" Asha wondered.

"Well, for starters, it's huge! I don't even know why you would call this an attic. You should call it the sky room or something," Jamal said with a giggle.

"The sky room?" Asha repeated with a confused look on her face.

"Yeah, because you can watch the sky change. I'm ecstatic about that! If I were you, I would be up here all the time," Jamal said.

Asha went over to stand next to him. "Well, believe it or not, I used to come up here a lot as a child to watch the sky change. I would watch the sunrise and sunset every day. But there's more to my kingdom than just this attic."

"Oh yeah, I figured that; you have to excuse me. You see, back home, I live in a condo, and we're just surrounded by street lights, buildings, and stores. We don't ever come across someone who lives in a palace!" Jamal explained.

"Understood. So you're a person who loves the sky, huh?" Asha asked.

"Oh yeah, I love the sky! It's the reason I started doing photography. There's no limit when it comes to taking pictures of the sky because it constantly changes. For some reason, it has always made me want to go out and see the rest of the world," Jamal said wistfully.

At that moment, Asha realized that she and Jamal shared a connection. She couldn't figure out how or why yet, but she knew that the connection was there.

As their conversation ended, they both stood up, hesitating slightly. They stared into each other's eyes as the moon was reflected upon their faces. "Oh—here's a blanket for you," Asha finally said, breaking the silence.
Jamal smirked as he grabbed the blanket that Asha handed him. "Thank you," he replied.

Meanwhile, Halima and Tamir were talking about the waterfall incident. "Yup, that's what happened: this big boulder moved and we fell right down the waterfall. There were sharks trying to attack us and everything! I nearly peed myself," Tamir told her.

Halima could not stop laughing at Tamir's story. She was laughing so hard that she had tears running down her face. "You've got to be kidding me! You two are hilarious!" she gasped as she wiped her face.

Asha suddenly appeared over Halima's shoulder. "Come on, Halima—let's give the boys their rest," she said as she lifted Halima off the ground.

"Okay, goodnight, boys!" Halima called.

"Goodnight!" Jamal and Tamir replied.

"We'll be downstairs in my room if you need us," Asha told them as she and Halima climbed out of the attic.

After closing the attic door, Halima gave Asha a suspicious look. "What is it now?" Asha demanded.

"You like him... I can tell you do," Halima answered with a smirk.

"No! I think he's cute, but I don't know him enough to say that I like him," Asha told her.

"Yeah, whatever!" Halima said while walking away.

"Hey, not so fast! It seems like you have a little crush on Tamir," Asha teased, catching up.

"Please—I wouldn't call it a crush. I just think he's cute, that's all," Halima responded sarcastically, mocking her friend.

Up in the attic, Jamal and Tamir were also talking about their new acquaintances. "Asha seems pretty cool," Tamir was saying.

"Yeah. I feel like she and I have a good connection," Jamal agreed.

"I feel the same way about Halima, but these girls probably have men in their lives already," Tamir said sadly.

"Hey, you never know—they probably have little crushes on us," Jamal told him, grinning.

Tamir started giggling. "Nah, bro, these girls are royalty. We'd be in way over our heads to think that. Trust me, they only see us as friends—that's it," he replied.

"Yeah, I guess you're right," Jamal agreed.

CHAPTER SIX

THE JOURNEY BEGINS

The next morning, Asha crawled up to the attic and caught Jamal staring at the sunrise. "Wow, you're a man of your word," she exclaimed.

Shocked, Jamal turned around. "Oh, hey—I didn't hear you come in. What do you mean?" he asked.

"You really do love the sky! You were telling the truth," Asha replied.

"Oh yeah, I wouldn't lie about that. And for some reason, the sunrise seemed more special today than usual," Jamal told her.

"Maybe it's because you've never had a view like this before," Asha said as she smiled, looking out the interior window.

Suddenly, Halima burst into the attic, carrying a fruit basket. "Hey guys! I know you're hungry, so I brought up some breakfast!" she called.

"Thank you! I'm starving," Jamal said. He then turned to Tamir and began tapping his shoulder to wake him up. "Hey Tamir, wake up. Halima brought us some breakfast."

Sitting up, Tamir yawned and stretched. "Hmmm...where? Is it pancakes, bacon, and sausage?"

Halima frowned and huffed, "No!"

"No? Then what is it?" Tamir asked.

Halima pushed the fruit basket over toward him. "It's fruit! Look, we have mangos, pineapples, oranges, apples, peaches, bananas, and kiwi."

Tamir didn't say a word, he just stared at the basket with a look of disgust.

Asha quickly intervened. "Is the breakfast fine for you two to eat?" she asked.

"Yes, this is great. We love eating fruit," Jamal said. "This is cool with you, right, Tamir?"

"I guess," Tamir replied nonchalantly.

"What is this bacon and sausage you speak of?" Halima asked as she bit into a peach.

"It's meat that we cook in America," Tamir answered in an aggravated tone as he took an apple.

"Oh—it sounds disgusting," Halima said, right before taking another bite of her peach again.

In that moment of awkward silence, Halima and Tamir began to smile at each other.

Seconds later, they heard a sudden knock from downstairs. Asha swiftly left the attic and ran to her bedroom door. When she opened it, she saw Queen Naomi. "Hello, mother!" she said cheerfully.

"Good morning, Asha... Listen, I just wanted to tell you that your father and I weren't upset with you yesterday. We just want what's best for you, that's all," Queen Naomi explained.

As Queen Naomi continued to talk, Asha didn't really pay attention to what was being said because she was too concerned about what was going on in the attic and getting caught.

"Asha! Are you listening to what I'm saying?" Queen Naomi demanded.

"Yes, mother, I understand everything you're telling me. I'm just a little tired, that's all. I'm going to take a nap now, okay?" Asha replied with a fake yawn.

"All right, honey. I'm glad you understand. Love you!" the queen answered.

"Love you too, mother!" Asha told her as she shut the door.

She then climbed back to the attic and closed the attic door firmly. "Who was that?" Halima asked.

"It was just my mother checking up on me."

"Is everything okay?" Jamal wondered.

"Yes, everything is fine. Thanks for asking," Asha confirmed.

"So, where are we going today?" Jamal asked.

"We are going to take you two flying in the Buggiez," Asha said.

"Buggiez—what's that?" Tamir piped in.

"You'll see," Asha replied mysteriously.

Halima quickly removed the leftover fruit from the basket and pulled out two white t-shirts with red, black, and green stripes on them and two white pants with gold sandals. "Before we do anything, we have to get you guys dressed," she said as she handed the clothes to Jamal and Tamir.

"These are the clothes we saw the people wearing outside," Tamir said.

"Exactly! We have to keep you two under the radar so that the citizens won't grow suspicious. If you keep the clothes you have on now, you guys would easily stand out," Asha explained.

A few minutes later, Jamal and Tamir had gotten dressed and climbed down from the attic with Asha and Halima. They then met up with Asha's pet elephant Dayo at the front door. "All right, come on, guys—get into the basket like you did before," Halima said as she climbed onto Dayo's back.

41

Tamir gave Halima a shady look. "What now, Tamir?" she demanded.

"I thought we wouldn't have to hide anymore now that we have these royal uniforms on," Tamir answered.

"I'm not taking that risk while we're here at the main palace. You may be dressed like the people here, but they still don't know who you are," Halima said.

"But if people do end up seeing you, we'll tell them that you're our classmates from school. Hopefully, that will throw them off for a while," Asha explained.

"Okay, cool, that's understandable," Jamal replied agreeably.

As they began to ride Dayo, Asha, and Halima made a slight change of plans. "You know what? Before we get on the Buggiez, I think it's time that we introduce you to some of the animals at our nature park," Asha said.

"NO!" Jamal and Tamir shouted.

Halima slapped the basket. "Shush! Don't shout! You're hiding, remember," she whispered. "Now, why don't you two want to visit our animals?"

"I am not trying to have the same incident from yesterday happen again," Tamir whispered back.

Asha giggled, "Oh, you will be fine. They no longer see you as trespassers, and you're with us, so they'll treat you with love," she said.

"I'm so scared, man," Tamir hissed to Jamal.

"Me too, bro, but we can trust them...I think," Jamal replied.

Dayo walked them from the palace all the way to the kingdom's nature park. After entering the park, Asha and Halima climbed off of Dayo and checked to see if anyone was around. "It's clear over here," Asha said.

"It's clear on this side as well," Halima added, coming from the opposite side.

"All right, guys, you can come out!" Asha called.

Jamal and Tamir were still a little frightened and refused to leave the basket. "Let's just act like we're sleeping, bro!" Tamir whispered fiercely. "Pretend you're asleep!"

"Oh come on, boys, I promise you'll be safe now," Halima told them.

"They're giving us their word. We'll be fine, man," Jamal told Tamir.

When Jamal and Tamir hopped out of the basket, they were mesmerized by their surroundings. They saw giraffes eating from trees, monkeys swinging from vines, and hippos swimming in ponds. One side of the park was filled with acres of grassland. The other side was loaded with jungle, waterfalls, and tree houses. "This place is so amazing! I see there are a lot of tree houses here. What are they here for?" Jamal wondered.

"It's for the kids. This is usually where the children play, but they're all at school right now," Asha answered.

"They have school on weekends?" Tamir asked.

"Yes, the kids here have school every day! Didn't you have school every day as a kid?" Halima asked Tamir.

"No, not at all. If that were the case, I wouldn't have went to school," Tamir answered with a grin.

Halima rolled her eyes. "Oh my, you're a sad case."

After getting adjusted to his surroundings, Tamir started to feel a little more comfortable and decided to go explore. "I'm going to check out one of the tree houses," he told the others as he started to climb one of the ladders.

Out of nowhere, Azi came running through the grass to greet Halima and Asha. Halima noticed that he had a note for her attached to his collar. She quickly grabbed it before Jamal and Asha noticed. She saw that the note was from Namdi, saying sorry about the other night.

"What are you reading?" Asha asked as Halima caught her attention.

"Oh nothing, just crap," Halima said as she rapidly tore the paper into tiny pieces, letting it blow away in the wind.

"Oh, okay," Asha answered, taking her mind off the

matter. "Hey Jamal, meet Azi!" she called.

Jamal started petting Azi. "Cute lion. How old is he?" he asked.

"Azi is four months old with a lot of energy," Asha answered, while petting the cub. "Isn't that right, boy? Where are your momma and poppa, Azi?"

Right after Asha's question, Azi's mother and father, Afia and Asad, came walking up the hill toward them. When Jamal saw Asad and Afia, his heart started racing and he began to slowly back up behind Asha. "Girls, are you sure Asad won't attack me this time?" he asked with a trembling voice.

"Yes, you're fine, Jamal. Go pet him. You'll see," Asha said as she gave Jamal a little shove closer to Asad. Jamal walked over to Asad with fear in his eyes and his hands shaking. "Hey Asad, long time, no see... I didn't know you had a wife and kid."

Asad just continued to give Jamal a straight-faced look. "Oh, okay, no laughs. Well, of course you're not going to laugh, you're a lion, for Christ's sake. Um, I don't know what else to say now, so I'm going to pet you, okay?" Jamal babbled.

When Asad allowed Jamal to pet him and Afia, Jamal sighed in relief and realized that there was nothing to be afraid of. "You see, I told you they would like you!" Asha told him with a smirk.

Before he could reply, they all heard screams coming from the closest tree house. "AW MAN, OH NO!" Tamir yelled as he attempted to jump down from the tree.

A gorilla in the tree house quickly grabbed Tamir by the collar of his shirt before he could fall to the ground. Right after that, a little boy poked his head out of the tree house and looked down at Asha, Halima, and Jamal. "I told him he wouldn't hurt him!" the boy protested.

Halima gasped and couldn't believe what she was seeing. "Zane! What are you doing here? Why aren't you at school?" she demanded.

"I told my parents I felt sick today. Please don't tell them you saw me here. I just wanted to play with Jojo and Nailah."

"All right, but we are going to take you back home when we leave. We wouldn't want someone else to catch you. You could really get in serious trouble!" Asha told Zane.

"Ugh...okay," Zane agreed.

As the gorilla held onto Tamir's shirt, Tamir kept screaming for dear life. "HE'S GOING TO KILL ME, I KNOW IT. ASHA, HALIMA—HELP ME! OH MY GOD, IS THAT ASAD I SEE DOWN THERE? MY LIFE IS OVER AS WE SPEAK!"

"Jojo's not going to hurt you. He's trying to save you from getting hurt. That's a big drop, ya know," Zane said as he jumped onto Jojo's back. "Come on, Jojo, let's take this crybaby to his friends."

Jojo climbed out of the tree house with Zane on his back and Tamir on his left arm. Zane's pet cheetah Nailah elusively climbed down the tree behind them. After that, Jojo gently placed Tamir on the grass near Halima's feet. Halima then put her hands on her hips. "You need to thank Jojo!" she demanded. "While you were thinking he was going to harm you, he actually saved your life!"

"Thank you, Jojo. I'm sorry about how I reacted. I'm just not used to seeing gorillas, especially up this close," Tamir told Jojo apologetically.

"And what about Nailah?" Zane asked.

"Sorry, Nailah. I've never been this close to a cheetah before, either," Tamir said as he petted her. Tamir then spotted Asad. "Hello, Asad," he murmured. "I'm guessing we're all good now, right?"

"Yeah, man, Asad is actually really nice," Jamal said as the lion licked his face.

"Okay, cool, cool—just checking!" Tamir replied.

Zane suddenly gave Asha a mischievous look. "Why are you staring at me like that, Zane?" Asha wondered. Zane didn't respond; he just kept staring. "Zane!" she said sternly.

"What's on your mind, child?" Halima asked the boy.

"Who are those guys?" Zane asked.

"They're our classmates from school. We're working on a project," Asha replied.

"But I've never met them before. I don't even recognize them. Did you see how the one guy reacted toward Jojo? No one who lives here is scared of the animals like that guy is; and there's no way you're working on a project because school is already over for college students."

Halima and Asha started to panic because Zane was onto them. "Well, why are they wearing the royal attire, then?" Halima asked the boy.

"Yeah, I see that they are wearing the royal attire, but...they aren't from here, are they?" Zane wondered.

Asha and Halima gave in and finally decided to tell Zane the truth. "Okay, look, Zane, you can't tell anyone about this, all right?" Asha said.

"That's right," Halima added. "If you can keep your mouth shut, we won't tell your parents you skipped school today."

"Okay, fair enough. I won't say a word," Zane agreed.

Suddenly, they all heard the sound of drums and tambourines being played and people singing a few miles away. "Where is that music coming from?" Jamal asked.

"It's coming from the elders at the Matana Center. Instead of retiring and lying down all day, some decide to help babysit the infants, some become assistant teachers, and the rest play music every morning to get the day started," Asha explained.

Jamal, who was sitting near the base of a tree, watched as Tamir, Halima, and Zane started randomly holding hands, twirling, and dancing to the music in a constant circle. Asha then put her hand out toward Jamal. "Come on, let's dance," she said.

"Okay!" Jamal replied as he grabbed her hand and began to dance.

"Nice footwork! I see you're a great dancer, too!" Asha told him.

"Nah, you're the great dancer. I'm just all right, but I have seen a couple African dances on TV, so I know a little something-something," Jamal said after twirling Asha and dipping her.

After the elders stopped playing music, Asha and Halima were prepared to leave and called Dayo for a ride. "All right, Zane, come ride with us. It's time to take you home," Halima said as she helped him climb on top of Dayo.

Zane seemed kind of sad that he had to leave. "Oh, okay... Bye, Jojo; bye, Nailah. I'll see ya tomorrow," he said.

As Dayo pulled up in front of Zane's palace, Asha and Halima walked him to the door. "Now, Zane, don't do this ever again, okay? You can play with Jojo and Nailah every day during recess or after school," Asha told Zane as she opened the door for him.

"All right, I won't ever do it again. Thanks for the ride, girls," Zane replied as he hugged Asha and Halima.

Next, Dayo took them all the way to the top of a cliff. On this cliff, there were hundreds of gold flying machines parked on the grass. The royal people called these gold flying machines Buggiez because they looked like bugs with wings.

"All right, we're finally here. Jamal, you're going to ride with me, and Tamir's going to ride with Halima," Asha said as she and Halima hopped onto two different Buggiez.

"Make sure you hang onto me when we start to fly. If you don't, you'll fall off," Halima told Tamir.
"Say no more!" Tamir replied as he quickly grabbed onto to her.

As soon as Asha and Halima gripped the handles, the Buggiez began to float in the air. Jamal started to feel butterflies in his stomach. "Wow, we're actually about to fly," Jamal thought to himself with a huge grin on his face.

"Hold on tight!" Asha told Jamal as they took off.

"Holding on!" Jamal replied.

Asha and Halima flew Jamal and Tamir all around Matana Kingdom to show them where everything was. During the flight, Asha pointed toward a massive building. "Over here, we have the Matana School. It starts with preschool and ends with college," she told Jamal as they flew over it.

"No wonder this building looks like an entire city. Speaking of school, I heard you graduated recently," Jamal said.

This caught Asha by surprise. "Hey, how do you know that?"

"A man named Mr. Kwame told me; he was our tour guide at the resort," Jamal explained.

"Oh, Mr. Kwame. Wow, he's a tour guide too? I swear

that old man has a million jobs—but yeah, I graduated last week," Asha replied.

"Wow! How coincidental! I'm actually graduating from college this upcoming week," Jamal told her.

"That's great! What's the name of your school?" she asked.

"City University. It's not as big as your school, though," Jamal answered.

"Shoot—I don't think any school on the planet is as big as their school," Tamir called out jokingly.

As they continued to fly, Jamal saw a huge skyscraper standing out from the rest of the buildings surrounding it. "What's that tall building over there for?" he asked.

"That's Matana's Royal Headquarters. That is usually where my father works," Asha explained.

"Oh, okay—so, as the King of Matana, what does your father have to do?" Jamal wondered.

"Well, he has to make sure that our guards are being properly trained to keep trespassers away. He doesn't usually have to worry about that because the animals that roam around here do an awesome job protecting us. The guards are just back-up. He also makes sure that the citizens have plenty of food and money for their families. Even though he's a king, he treats all of our people with love," Asha explained.

"Wow! So what about your mother? What does she do?" Jamal asked.

"As the queen of Matana, my mother makes sure that the school is run well by keeping the teachers and students consistently in a great mood. She makes sure that the entire curriculum is taught with positive energy. Some days, she even surprises everyone at the school with gifts. Every day, the teachers look forward to teaching and the students look forward to learning, all because of my mother. The people here love her because she's a social butterfly. Oh yeah, one more thing: she also spends the other half of her day visiting families to make sure they're healthy and that their home lives are fine," Asha answered.

"Your parents are very kind-hearted people. It makes me wonder, though—how come non-royal people aren't allowed in the kingdom?" Jamal asked.

"Um...we'll talk about that later," Asha replied hesitantly. Jamal wondered why Asha wouldn't just answer his question at that moment.

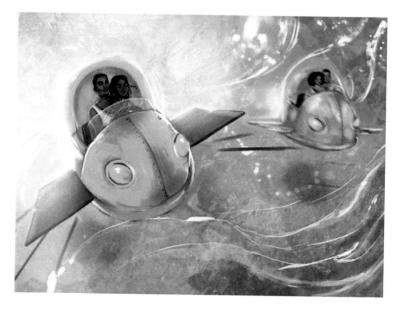

As they flew over the sea Jamal noticed that Asha and Halima were flying them closer to the water near a whirlpool. "Where are you taking us?" he asked.

"To show you more of the kingdom; we have a fun place to go underwater, too. It's called Matana Town," Asha replied.

As they hovered above the whirlpool, Asha and Halima pressed a button on the Buggiez that made the vehicles transform. Wall barriers began to rise on both sides of the Buggiez and large glass ceilings started to lift up from the fronts, stretching all the way to the backs. After their complete transformation, the Buggiez looked more like submarines.

After that, Asha and Halima flew them into the whirlpool, splashing into a tunnel filled with water. They traveled rapidly through the tunnel, moving up, down, and all around like on a roller coaster ride. "Yo! This is better than any ride I've ever been on!" Jamal shouted, enjoying himself immensely.

At the midsection of the tunnel, the current slowed down. In their Buggiez, Tamir decided to spark up a conversation with Halima to break the silence. "So, Halima...what's your whole role, here?" he asked.

"What do you mean, my role?" Halima repeated.

"I mean, you aren't a princess, but I know you're attached to this royal family somehow. So what are you?" he asked.

"Well, first of all, everyone here is considered royal, since we are the only descendants from the Royal Matana people that built this entire kingdom. Let me just break down this entire thing for you," Halima answered while continuing to fly. "Now, ya see, Asha is my best friend. We're like sisters, and I do my best to make sure she always stays on the right path. Being Asha's best friend is my role when it comes to the royal family.

"My father Hakim is second in command to King Juma, and he helps him with the overseeing and decision-making for the good of the kingdom. Everyone calls my father Chancellor Hakim. My mother, Iman, plays a supportive role with helping Asha's mother keep the homes and school running smoothly and being well-organized. She is known as Lady Iman, but she likes it when everyone just calls her Iman. I'll be taking over her job whenever Asha becomes queen. What we do is very important because if anything were to ever happen to the King and Queen, God forbid, my parents would have to take over. I don't even like thinking about that because we all love each other like one big family," Halima finished.

"Damn, sorry for my ignorance. You do play a big a role here," Tamir said.

"It's all right—you're just a city boy. You don't know any better," Halima teased.

When they arrived at the end of the tunnel, Jamal and Tamir noticed that it had led them to a city that was protected by a huge glass perimeter. It looked like a giant snow globe, but with real people inside. "Yo, is this Matana Town? How much money did it cost to create this place?" Jamal asked, awed.

"It didn't cost my ancestors a dime to make this place. They created Matana Town centuries ago," Asha explained with a smile.

"Wow! I just can't believe what I'm seeing right now," Jamal said.

Halima noticed that there were a lot of people in the town and wanted to make sure that she and Asha didn't get caught bringing in strangers. "Tamir, make sure you crouch down a bit when we go inside, okay? We have to take precautions," she said.

"But I want to see what's going on," Tamir whined.

"I understand that, you big baby. That's why I told you to crouch down just a tad bit!" Halima reiterated.

Since Asha and Halima were in separate Buggiez and underwater, the only way that they could communicate with each other was by using walkie-talkies. "Asha, there are a lot of people here. Make sure you tell Jamal to crouch down once we enter the town. I just told Tamir to do the same thing," Halima said into her walkie-talkie.

"Wow, they must've all come while we were at the nature park. All right, I'll let him know," Asha replied. "Did you hear that?" she asked, turning off the walkie-talkie and turning to Jamal.

"Yup, I'm crouching now," Jamal replied.

As the entrance to Matana Town opened up, Jamal and Tamir witnessed hundreds of people flying on the Buggiez. The town looked like an ancient civilization and a futuristic city combined. There were buildings, temples, shrines, and restaurants all over the place.

As they entered the town, Asha and Halima started to fly with the speedy flow of traffic. To Jamal and Tamir, this experience was surreal. It felt like they were on a virtual ride at a theme park. They then felt the momentum of the Buggiez decreasing. Peeking through the windows, they saw plenty of Buggiez just hovering in the air, waiting in a line.

"What's going on?" Tamir wondered as the Buggiez continued to move slowly.

"Well, you didn't seem too fond of breakfast this morning, so we thought you would at least like lunch," Halima said as they flew up to a seafood restaurant.

"Yes!" Tamir boasted. "Is that seafood I smell? Finally, real food!" He turned to Halima. "I thought you didn't eat meat."

"It isn't meat, it's seafood," Halima answered.

Tamir looked very confused. "But it is..."

"HUSH!" Halima said, cutting Tamir off. "It's healthier than the food you eat."

"Okay, yeah, you're right!" Tamir responded with a grin.

"All right, now keep quiet. We're getting closer to the Fly-Thru window, and I'm about to take our order," Halima told him.

"Fly-Thru? What's that? Ohhh...like drive-thru. That's clever!" Tamir whispered to himself.

"Hello, Halima. What will you be having today?" one of the workers asked as Halima flew up to the window.

"Hello. I'll just have the fish and shrimp meal, please, with a large mango frosty," Halima answered.

"All right, here ya go. Have a nice day," the worker said as she placed the food in the side vent of the Buggie.

After ordering their food, Asha and Halima flew the boys into a building that had plenty of personal garages/dine-in rooms for parking and eating. After Asha and Halima parked the Buggiez, Jamal and Tamir hopped out and looked around the private dine-in room. There was one long picnic table in the middle of the room and a window on the opposite side of the room that showed an interior view of the ocean. "This place is amazing! So what else is there to do around here besides eat sea food?" Jamal wondered as they sat down to eat.

"A lot of things. We can go swimming in the cave, eat sea food again, take you to see some of the temples, or watch the water show where the dolphins and whales do tricks together," Asha told him.

"We can do all of that today?" Jamal asked excitingly.

"Yes!" Asha answered with enthusiasm.

"I see you're enjoying Matana's seafood," Halima said while watching Tamir stuff his face with fish and shrimp.

"The food here is okay, I guess. It would've been better

if it were fried instead of baked," Tamir replied with a smirk on his face, teasing her.

Halima began to laugh hysterically. "Oh, you're killing me! I just can't win with you!" she said as she punched him in the shoulder.

After eating lunch, Jamal and Tamir thought that Asha and Halima were going to take them to see one of Matana's water shows. When they flew past the show, Tamir immediately said, "Woah! Woah! Woah! I thought we were going to the show! What's going on?"

"Yeah, about that... Um, we actually can't take you to see the water show. It's too much of a risk because a lot of people will be there, and it's a sit-in event. That would expose you guys to way too much attention," Halima explained.

"Well, I wish you would've told us that earlier," Tamir said, disappointed.

"I know. I'm sorry. We forgot to tell you after we talked about it during lunch. We thought that you two wearing the royal attire would help people not notice you, but Zane obviously proved us wrong on that one," the girl said.

Tamir started laughing as he understood where Halima was coming from. "Yeah, he definitely did," he agreed.

"But hey, don't worry—we have something much better planned. We're going to take you to see one of our sea caves. It's going to be way more fun!" Halima told him happily.

Asha and Halima flew them out of Matana Town, but they remained traveling in the sea. The Buggiez plunged quickly through the water and into a cave, surfacing in a pocket of air. After Asha and Halima parked in the cave, they climbed out and ran toward a pool.

"Come on in!" Halima told Jamal and Tamir as she dove in with Asha.

As Tamir and Jamal were stepping out of the Buggiez,

they noticed that the water in the pool had a glow that illuminated the cave. It looked like nature's own Jacuzzi. The rocks in the cave were glistening and reflecting brightly off the water. There was also a huge sculpture of a head right above the pool with water coming out of its mouth and glowing eyes.

"That sculpture looks eerie. I feel like it's staring directly at me," Jamal said.

"It may look eerie to you, but it represents divinity. It was made to show the people that the creator would never stop providing us with the resources that we need. I believe this was one of the first sculptures my ancestors made," Asha explained as she swam.

"That's enough of the history lessons for now," Halima said.

"Yeah," Asha agreed. "Are you guys coming in or not?"

"We're coming!" Jamal told her as he and Tamir dove into the pool at the same time.

"The water is really warm. This is just how I like it— the type of pool you could fall asleep in," Tamir said while doing backstrokes.

"Hey, so when is the fun stuff going to happen?" he asked a few minutes later.

"Oh, don't worry, its coming. You and Jamal stand right up there on that small cliff," Halima said while she and Asha climbed up the cliff as well.

"OH SOLOMON, COME HERE, BOY!" Halima shouted toward the pool once they were all on dry ground. About five seconds later, a big humpback whale came jumping out of the water and splashing back into it. Solomon then blew water out of his blowhole as he swam slightly above the pool's surface.

"Hello, Solomon. It looks like you're happy to see us," Asha cooed as she and Halima petted the whale. "Halima and I brought some friends with us today. Can they come swim with us?"

Solomon hummed in a calm way and nodded his head up and down, signaling yes. Jamal and Tamir were speechless as they witnessed Solomon comprehend what Asha and Halima was saying to him.

"Solomon is okay with taking you two for a swim," Halima said as she handed them gold objects shaped like noses.

"What are these?" Jamal asked, holding the object in his hand.

"These are called Nozzelz. Place them onto your nose like this. They will push oxygen into your nostrils, which will help you breathe while we're underwater," Asha explained.

After putting the Nozzelz on, they all sat on Solomon's back and prepared to travel underwater.

Solomon took them deep into the sea, and since they were now underwater without the Buggiez or walkie-talkies, they could no longer speak to each other. Moments later, it became so dark that they could no longer see each other, either. All they could do was hang onto Solomon. The sounds of the sea and Solomon's gentle swimming made the experience a lot more peaceful and magical than Jamal thought it would be, though.

Further into the sea, Jamal noticed that they were headed to a certain spot that had a magic glow. As Solomon swam closer to the strange light, Jamal and Tamir saw that it was coming from glowing jellyfish.

Asha then took Jamal by the hand to allow him to get a closer look at the jellyfish. As they slowly floated off of the whale, they treaded water and watched a swarm of glowing jellyfish swim all around them. As the neon lights reflected onto Asha, Jamal was captivated by her beauty. "Aw man, I think I'm falling in love with this girl," he thought to himself. "Snap out of it, Jamal—she's out of your league. She's a freaking princess."

After Jamal snapped out of his daze, Asha grabbed his hand and swam back to Solomon. Solomon then took them through a huge tunnel where they could see the sunlight beaming into the sea. The tunnel led to a colorful part of the sea that was full of life. They swam through a school of fish, frolicked with dolphins, observed coral reefs blow constant bubbles, and watched clownfish hide in sea anemones.

After having fun in the sea, Solomon took them back to the cave. As they climbed out of the water and onto the cliff, they took the Nozzelz off of their noses and thanked the whale for the incredible time they'd had. "Man, I want to live here! Do you two get to do things like this all the time?" Jamal asked.

"Yes, but we've never been in the water that long before. I guess you and Tamir made it way more fun this time,"

Asha answered.

"Well, we're glad to be acquaintances," Tamir said.

"And I really wish I had my camera, especially when the jellyfish came," Jamal added.

"It's okay. Just retain that image in your brain, and it will become an important memory," Asha told him.

"I will to have to retain everything I've seen on this trip, I guess," Jamal said as he and Tamir began to walk toward the Buggiez.

"Stop right there! You two aren't getting in the Buggiez soaking wet," Halima scolded.

"Then where are we supposed to go?" Tamir asked.

Halima pointed at a tunnel toward the right side of the cave. "Right over there in that windy tunnel. It will dry you off within seconds."

When they all walked into the tunnel, the powerful wind instantly dried their clothes. "Wow, that was quick!" Tamir said, feeling his clothes.

"Told ya," Halima answered smugly.

They then hopped onto the Buggiez and flew out of the sea. As they flew above the sea and into the sky, Jamal could see the sun glaring directly back at them; it was almost as if they were flying into the sun.

CHAPTER SEVEN

THE BATTLE OF MATANA

"Jamal, look ahead! Do you see the statues over there?" Asha asked as she pointed to a gigantic figure in the distance.

"Yeah, who is that?" Jamal asked.

"That's a statue of my ancestor, Queen Asha. She was my great-great-great-great-great-grandmother, and, as you can see, I am named after her," Asha revealed.

"Yeah, I see. So why did they make a statue of her?" Jamal wondered.

"They did it to honor her for winning the Battle of Matana," Asha said.

"The Battle of Matana . . . When did that happen?" Jamal asked.

"Well, it's coming up on its 500-year anniversary. What took place that day was joyful and horrific at the same time."

"How? You don't mind telling me the story do you?" Jamal asked.

"No, I don't mind," Asha replied. "On that day two evil leaders, Zimmer and Zelda, and their soldiers—or invaders—finished destroying most of the kingdoms on our continent. They stole everyone's gold, took all of our diamonds, and wiped out most of our food reserves. You see, Zimmer and Zelda came from a place that was constantly freezing. They lacked food, water, and other resources needed for survival. I believe living in those poor conditions caused Zimmer, Zelda, and the rest of the invaders to be evil. These people never knew how to spread love and share. They only knew how to hate and take. As soon as they became brave enough to leave their environments, they looted and killed everywhere they went.

"And 500 years ago it was different here. Anyone was allowed to walk in and out of Matana kingdom. Our people welcomed everyone with opened arms. My ancestors taught us that we should always greet our fellow human beings with love. We weren't used to being violent or selfish because we never had to be.

"Remember when you asked me how come non-royal people aren't allowed in the kingdom?" Asha asked Jamal.

"Yeah," Jamal answered.

"Well, this story will answer your question," Asha
said.

"I'm listening," Jamal replied. He relaxed on the
Buggie while Asha flew them in circles around the statue.

"At this time King Yoba and Queen Asha, who are my
great-great-great-great-great-grandparents by the way,
provided plenty of wealth and food for anyone who needed
it. So on the day of the invasion, the invaders tricked my
ancestors by greeting them in a kind way. They pretended
they wanted to be companions and learn about our way of
life. When really, they were only there to figure out the
secret to our power source so they could steal it."

"Sorry to cut you off, but what generates the power
source here?" Jamal asked.

"The spirit energy is our power source. Do you see the
magical-looking ball of light hovering above the statue's
hand?" Asha asked Jamal.

"Yeah, I see it," Jamal answered.

"That's the spirit energy. It holds the spiritual energy of
all Matana's ancestors. This helps power up the lights, heat,
and Matana Town. It even powers up the Buggiez to fly."

"So that's why the invaders wanted the spirit energy,"
Jamal said.

"Yes, now back to the story," Asha said. "When King
Yoba greeted Zimmer and Zelda at the front gates, he
allowed them to enter. Immediately after he let them in, the
invaders raided our kingdom. Zimmer pulled out a gun and
shot and killed King Yoba in front of Queen Asha and their
children. The citizens of Matana instantly ran to King
Yoba's aid and tried to save him. Most of the men tried to
fight back the invaders, but they were no match for their
guns and explosives. The invaders began to kill everyone in
sight while stealing our gold, silver, and diamonds.

"Though she was shocked by her husband's death,
Queen Asha tried to stay strong. She and most of the
women who were alive hid the children at the school. As

Queen Asha continued to weep, she suddenly heard King Yoba's voice behind her. When she turned around she saw him standing there in a graceful spirit form. She realized she could touch and hold him again, but she still felt a mix of joy and sorrow. Tears continued to flow down her cheeks as King Yoba held her in his arms and told her they didn't have much time. He said they needed to call on their ancestors for support.

"With King Yoba's newly refined spirit and Queen Asha's human flesh, they established a strong connection to the spirit world. The ancestors answered their calls almost immediately and sent down a power so strong that even mother nature began to fight the invaders. The invaders started being struck by lightning and swept away by heavy winds and tornadoes.

"Before disappearing, King Yoba gave Queen Asha one last hug and kiss. He told her he would be fighting with her in spirit and would see her again in the afterlife. After he disappeared, he passed on the rest of his spirit energy, along with the ancestors' spirit energy, to her. She felt the power of her ancestors running through her veins, and her eyes began to glow and become fully gold. With golden spirit energy hovering in the palms of her hands, she flew out of the school and began to blast each invader with bursts of energy, killing them one by one.

"Zimmer realized that the invaders were quickly losing the battle, so he and the few invaders left pulled in their loaded cannons. Zelda then brought out some of the elders and held them at gunpoint. Hoping that Queen Asha would finally surrender and tell them where to find the power source, Zimmer threatened to bomb the entire kingdom, and Zelda threatened to kill the elders.

"But Queen Asha did not back down. She told them that the power source is not something that you can just take; it is something that you must earn. Zelda was disgruntled and told Zimmer to light the cannons. With the help of the ancestors, Queen Asha quickly used her power to set off a blast that spread around the entire kingdom. The energy blast killed Zimmer and the invaders, and it left Zelda gravely injured. As Zelda laid on the ground, she still had one more evil task up her sleeves. In her last breath, she told the Queen that she had put a curse on Matana and that she and Zimmer would be back stronger than ever in 500 years to obtain the power source.

"But thanks to the blast Queen Asha set off, the power source was much stronger. Matana was easily restored, and all of the royal citizens were healed. Queen Asha and the rest of the royal citizens closed off Matana from the rest of society so that a travesty could never happen again. To protect the kingdom they built a military, which is why you always see guards walking around," Asha explained.

"What about the curse? Isn't the 500-year anniversary coming soon? And whatever happened with Queen Asha?" Jamal asked.

"I've been told that Queen Asha prophesized that the curse would not happen as long as her great-great-great-great-great-granddaughter marries the man chosen for her by the ancestors. If she does not marry him, the curse will take over Matana, and Zimmer and Zelda will return once again. I don't believe in the curse or the prophecy though. I think every generation just panics every time the anniversary of the battle comes around.

"And to answer your second question, Queen Asha died of old age. It's been said that she smiled after her last breath because King Yoba was there spiritually, ready to take her to the afterlife," Asha said.

"Wow. So even though all of that happened, you still don't believe in the curse or the prophecy?" Jamal asked.

"Nope. Because everything here is too perfect. Nothing bad ever happens here. The only time something crazy ever happens here is when people try to break into our kingdom and steal something. They never make it pass the front gates though because the animals end up killing them. You know what? I guess that's why I sensed you had good intentions and were trustworthy—because the animals didn't kill you. They just stalled by frightening you guys until Halima and I got there," Asha said.

"So what you're saying is that if Tamir and I had had bad intentions, we would've been killed?"

"Yup," Asha replied.

"Alright, well back to what I was saying before. How can you be surrounded by all of this magic and still not believe in the prophecy or curse? Or are you just choosing not to believe it?" Jamal questioned.

Asha frowned, took the Buggie off autopilot, and quickly began to fly up into the clouds.

"Whoa did I say something wrong?" Jamal asked as he fell backwards onto his seat from the momentum. Asha became teary-eyed as she thought about the curse and the prophecy, and Jamal noticed a tear fall down the side of her face.

"Are you okay?" Jamal asked as he touched her shoulder.

"Don't look at me!" she shouted, embarrassed that Jamal saw her crying.

"Sorry," Jamal said, looking up and twiddling his fingers.

After a moment of awkward silence, Asha began to speak again. "Jamal," she said gently.

"Is it safe for me to answer?" Jamal asked.

"Yes," Asha said as she giggled and wiped away her tears. "I'm sorry, I didn't mean to snap at you. It's just that this curse and prophecy thing has really been a strain on my life. My parents have already chosen a man to be my prince too." Asha rolled her eyes in disgust.

"They believe he was chosen by the ancestors because blah-blah-blah and all that other nonsense, but he's far from the chosen one," she said.

"Oh really? What's his name?" Jamal asked with a gloomy face.

"Yoba," Asha replied, rolling her eyes again.

"Oh okay, well, he has the same name as your ancestor. How do you know that he isn't the chosen one?"

"I can just feel it. I know he isn't the one for me. I know his family just named him Yoba on purpose to make it seem like we were meant to be together. And it doesn't help that we were born in the same year and month either," Asha explained.

"Well what are you going to do?" Jamal asked.

"I don't know yet. I'm still trying to figure that part out."

"Jamal," Asha said again gently.

"Yeah what's up?" he replied.

"Did you really see my face in the sky?" she asked. Jamal giggled. "Yeah it was definitely you alright . . . Why?"

"Just wondering that's all," Asha said with a smirk on her face. "Let me show you where my parents, grandparents, great-grandparents, and the rest of my ancestors got married over the past 500 years."
She flew to the base of the statue, and they hopped off the Buggie. As they stood on the base, the statue's eyes lit up, but Jamal and Asha didn't notice.

"So this is where the magic happens, huh?" Jamal asked.

"Yup, this is where it happens," Asha replied. "They just hold hands like this and say 'I do.'" She goofed around and held Jamal's hands.

At the same time, Halima rode past on her Buggie and noticed that the statue's eyes were lit up. But in a moment she blinked, and Asha and Jamal hopped back onto the Buggie. When she looked again the eyes were dark, and Halima assumed she had just been hallucinating.

CHAPTER EIGHT

A NIGHT TO REMEMBER

Later that day, an elderly woman named Miss Enu visited Matana's Headquarters to see King Juma. "Hello, King Juma and Chancellor Hakim, sorry to bother you," she said as she walked into the office.

"No problem, Miss Enu, what's on your mind?" King Juma asked.

She placed her cane on King Juma's desk and sat down on one of his office chairs. "Well, I was walking around the neighborhood earlier today, and I saw Asha and Halima flying their Buggiez with two boys I've never seen before. King Juma, I didn't recognize these guys at all; I have no clue who they were," she said.

King Juma and Chancellor Hakim were confused. "Are you sure you didn't recognize them? Were they wearing the royal uniforms?" King Juma asked.

"Yes, they were," Miss Enu answered.

Chancellor Hakim smiled in relief. "Miss Enu, it was probably Yoba and his friend Namdi hanging out with them. Maybe you didn't get a good glimpse, that's all." Miss Enu frowned. "King Juma and Chancellor Hakim, I know exactly what my grandson Yoba and his friend Namdi look like. Trust me, they were not the boys with Asha and Halima today," she replied.

King Juma and Chancellor Hakim could see the concern on Miss Enu's face. "Okay, Miss Enu, we will check on them as soon as our work is finished," King Juma told her.

She smiled. "Thank you, I was just looking out for my future granddaughter-in-law, that's all," Miss Enu said as she walked out.

Meanwhile, Asha and Halima were flying the Buggiez back to where they'd gotten them. "I hope you two enjoyed yourselves today," Halima said as they parked the Buggiez.

"We sure did, I wish we could do it again," Tamir replied.

"Aw no, tomorrow is your last day, isn't it?" Asha asked.

"Yes, unfortunately it is, but I can always keep in contact with you. Do you have a cellphone or an email address?" Jamal asked.

"Oh no, sorry, I don't even know what those are," Asha answered as she giggled. "We can send letters to each other. My father always picks up our mail from the resort. Do you write letters?"

"Nah, but I can start," Jamal replied.

"Shoot, it just hit me, our graduation ceremony is three days away," Tamir said.

"Wow, no more school for us, man, up next is just ... life," Jamal said, wondering if he was ready for whatever was coming next.

"It's about to get dark. We should be heading back to

the palace soon," Asha said.

Halima whistled. "Dayo! May you please give us a ride back to the palace."

Dayo trotted over to Asha, wearing the same big basket on his back he'd had before. "Hurry, hop in, guys. I hear people coming," Halima said.

Tamir and Jamal hopped into the basket just in time as two people came up the hill. As the people came closer, Asha realized they were Yoba and Namdi. "Hey, Asha, I've been looking for you all day. Were you still in the palace getting over your sickness or something?" Yoba asked.

Asha put on a fake smile and said, "Hey Yoba. No, I haven't been in the palace all day. I've just been hanging around here and there."

"Oh okay, well, my grandmother said she saw you hanging out with a couple of guys today. Now, what guy could you possibly have been hanging out with today who is more important than me?" Yoba asked.

"Zane!" Asha answered, smirking.

"Yeah, she must have seen me, Asha, and Zane earlier. We gave him a ride today after he got out of class, that's all," Halima added.

"That little man has better game than me. If he's able to get you two beautiful ladies to pick him up from school, then I have a lot to learn," Namdi said.

"Yes, you do!" Halima said sarcastically, rolling her eyes at Namdi.

"So Asha, do you want to hang out tonight? We can go to Matana Town, eat some fish, and catch a water show," Yoba said.

As Yoba continued to talk Asha's head off, Jamal and Tamir were whispering in the basket. "Do you see this? These guys look like superheroes. Man, now I don't have a chance in the world with Halima. We might as well pack our bags right now," Tamir told Jamal.

Jamal snickered. "Now this is coming from the same guy who told me we were in over our heads to think that these girls would like us. You're funny, man!" he said.

Meanwhile, Asha had grown tired of Yoba trying to convince her to hang out. "Oh sorry, I actually just left Matana Town, and I'm about to head home to get some sleep. But I'm sure you can hang out with some random girls at the resort like you do every night," she told Yoba while her arms were folded.

"Oh snap, it just got real!" Jamal whispered. Yoba hung his head in shame. "Look, I'm just having a little fun, that's all, those girls don't mean anything to me. But um ... we can just hang out tomorrow," he said as he lifted his head, standing there awkwardly.

Meanwhile, Namdi was staring at Halima with a smile. "Ew, Namdi, what are you staring at?" Halima asked him.

"You beautiful," Namdi answered as he caressed Halima's face.

"Man, that line was so corny!" Tamir whispered, watching from the basket.

"What's the basket for?" Yoba asked.

"Food," Asha replied shortly.

They were interrupted by King Juma and Chancellor Hakim, walking up the hill. "Well, hello, King Juma and Chancellor Hakim. What brings you up here?" Yoba asked.

"Oh, nothing, we're just walking around the kingdom checking up on things," Chancellor Hakim answered, patting Namdi on the back.

"So hey, girls, how have you been today?" King Juma asked.

"We've been good, Dad. We're actually about to head home, we've had a long day," Asha said.

"All right, sweetheart, I'll see you when I get home," King Juma replied.

"Okay, bye Dad, bye Chancellor," Asha said.

"I'll see you later Dad, goodbye King Juma," Halima said as she and Asha rode away on Dayo.

King Juma and Chancellor Hakim stayed behind to talk to Yoba and Namdi. "I think we have nothing to worry about. Maybe Miss Enu needs glasses," Chancellor Hakim told King Juma.

"Yes, maybe you're right, but I must double check," King Juma said. "Hey, were you guys with Asha and Halima all day today?" he asked Yoba and Namdi.

"Oh no sir, we were actually looking for them all day. Namdi and I came across them when we came up the hill to get a Buggie. So I've only seen them once today for a few minutes," Yoba explained.

King Juma looked disturbed. "I see," he said.

"Is everything okay?" Yoba asked.

"Oh yes, everything is fine, Yoba. You guys have a good night, okay?" King Juma replied.

"Hey, if it makes you feel any better, the only guy who hung out with them today was Zane. Lucky kid!" Namdi told the king, laughing.

"I wonder how they ran into Zane. My wife told me he didn't show up to school today," Chancellor Hakim told King Juma as they walked back down the hill.

"Let's pay Zane a little visit," King Juma said.

King Juma and Chancellor Hakim knocked at the front door of Zane's palace. "Hey, Mr. and Mrs. Boateng," King Juma said as Zane's parents opened the door.

"King ... Chancellor, come on in, what brings you two by?" Mr. Boateng said.

"Well, we just wanted to speak to Zane really quick, that's all," Chancellor Hakim told them.

Mrs. Boateng looked worried. "Oh no, did he do something wrong?" she asked.

"No, not at all, we just wanted to know if he's been out with Asha and Halima today," King Juma said.

"He probably wasn't, he's been home all day because he's feeling a little under the weather, but I'll call him down now. Zane!" Mr. Boateng called.

"Yes, dad!" Zane answered.

"Come down here, please!" Mr. Boateng said.

"All right," Zane said as he came running down the stairs. "What's wrong ... oh hey, King Juma and Chancellor Hakim."

"Hey, Zane, were you with Asha and Halima at all today?" Chancellor Hakim asked.

Zane tapped his chin, pretending to think.

"Zane, be honest now," Mrs. Boateng said.

"Oh yeah, I was. When I caught them flying by the house, I stopped them and asked if they could take me to get some more herbs to help me get over my sickness," Zane said.

"You never mentioned this to us," Mrs. Boateng said.

"I know, I'm sorry, Mother. It must've slipped my mind," Zane replied.

"That's okay, Zane, you're fine. Miss Enu thought she

saw Asha and Halima with strangers or trespassers earlier today," King Juma said as he laughed.

"Oh wow, that old woman really needs some glasses," Mr. Boateng said as he escorted the King and Chancellor out the door.

"Mom, Dad, I'll be in my room," Zane said as he ran upstairs. He snuck out through his bedroom window and found a stranded Buggie to fly to Asha and Halima's palace.

Meanwhile, in the attic, Halima could feel a strange tension between her and Tamir. "Are you okay? You've been pretty quiet since we came in." she said.

"I'm fine ... your boyfriend Namdi seems cool," Tamir told Halima as he took a sip of his mango frosty.

Halima gasped. "Namdi is not my boyfriend. He's just a flirt. Wait, are you jealous?"

Tamir squinted, shrugging his shoulders. "Jealous ... no, I'm not jealous. I barely even know you, why would I be jealous?"

Halima snickered. "Okay, Namdi isn't my type anyway. I like my men loyal."

A few minutes later, King Juma and Chancellor Hakim entered the main palace to finish their investigation. They wanted to be sure that Zane's story was correct. King Juma headed upstairs and knocked on Asha's bedroom door. "Asha, Halima, come here please," he demanded.

Asha and Halima were shocked when they heard the King at the door. "You guys keep quiet, we'll be right back." Asha said as she and Halima climbed down the attic ladder into the room. "Yes, Father?"

"Hey, so Yoba and Namdi told me that they didn't get a chance to hang out with you two today, and Miss Enu thinks that she saw you and Halima with two strangers earlier," King Juma said as he and Chancellor Hakim watched the girls suspiciously.

"Oh, no, Father, it ... uh," Asha said, unsure what to say next.

Zane arrived just in time. He was right outside Asha's window, hovering on a Buggie, and holding up cue cards. Only Asha and Halima could see him.

"I'm listening," King Juma said, noticing the girls were distracted.

Halima quickly read Zane's cue card. "Uh, we just took Zane to the store to get him some herbs," she said. Asha read the second cue card. "Yes, Father, he stopped us when we passed by his palace and told us he was sick, so we took him to the store to help him feel better."

The King and Chancellor smiled in relief. "Well, I'm glad you gals were there to help the little guy," Chancellor Hakim said as he and the King went downstairs. "Tell that lady she needs glasses," Halima told the King and Chancellor as she closed the door. Before the door had fully closed, King Juma saw that the attic door was wide open. He didn't say a word.

Asha ran to the window. "Oh my God, Zane, thank you so much! You really saved us!"

"Yes, thanks, Zane! I can't believe Miss Enu really saw us. She's so nosy!" Halima said.

"I know, I can't stand that lady either. Hey, you two owe me a mango frosty now," Zane said.

"All right, Zane, now go get some sleep, kid," Asha told him.

"Okay, bye girls!" Zane said as he flew away on the Buggie.

Suddenly there was a thump at the door. "Ugh, who is it this time?" Asha said as she opened it.

"It's Dayo! What do you have wrapped around your tusk, boy?" Halima said as she grabbed the objects off Dayo's tusk.

"You found them! These are Jamal and Tamir's

cameras, but I don't know what this other device is," Asha said. Admiringly, she scrolled through the photos on Jamal's camera. "Oh wow, he really did see my face in the sky, look!" Asha said as she found the magical picture Jamal had taken of her. "He told me they have this picture in the lobby at the resort as well."

"I can't believe I'm really seeing this ... Asha, do you think this may be a sign? Ya know, like a sign that the ancestors chose him to be your prince," Halima said.

"I don't know, possibly. I hope so," Asha said. Halima started clapping. "Yay, are you going to tell him!"

"No, are you crazy, that might scare him off," Asha said.

"Well, you're going to have to do it sooner than later," Halima said.

"I know," Asha said. "I'll do it when the time is right."

While waiting for Asha and Halima, Jamal and Tamir were talking in the attic. "Yo, Halima was telling me the story of Asha's ancestor, Queen Asha. That story was so crazy, man, I almost cried," Tamir said.

"I know, Asha told me the story too. It was a lot to take in," Jamal said.

"So, do you believe in that curse and prophecy thing?" Tamir asked.

"Yes, I believe it, especially because of all the unexplainable things we've seen," Jamal said. "Soooo, do you think she's going to marry Yoba?" Tamir asked.

"She told me she doesn't want to marry him, but I honestly think she has no choice," Jamal said. Asha and Halima returned to the attic, looking tense.

"Is everything okay?" Jamal said.

"We have to get you guys out of here early tomorrow morning. Yoba's grandmother Miss Enu is on to us, and I think she has my father a little concerned," Asha said.

"I'm sorry, Asha, I didn't mean to get you caught up in

all this mess," Jamal said.

"Don't worry, Jamal, it's not your fault. I just wish the people here could be more open minded," Asha said.

"I know. This sucks because I've really enjoyed getting to know you guys these past couple days," Halima said as she walked over to Tamir. "And Tamir, you're a really funny guy and a great person to be around."

"Thanks, you were a pain in the butt sometimes, but you definitely grew on me. I'm actually going to miss it here, including the food," Tamir said as he and Halima laughed together.

"Hey, we're going to stay up here with you guys tonight, okay? And oh, we have something for you two." Asha reached into her bag and pulled out Jamal and Tamir's cameras.

"Wow, you found them!" Jamal said joyfully.

"Yeah, Dayo must have found them a few hours ago. They were a little wet when he brought them to us, so we dried them off. Oh yeah, Dayo found something else too," Halima said, reaching into Asha's bag. "It's some weird device thingy." She gave it to Tamir.

"My phone! Thank God! Sit down with me, Halima, let me show you how a cellphone works," Tamir said as he turned it on. "Aw man, I can't get reception here, so I can't show you social media, but look, these are called apps, this is how you take a selfie, and this is how you enter a number to call someone." Tamir said, demonstrating.

"This is such a strange device. There is way too much going on here," Halima said, giggling.

"I could thank Dayo a million times, I am so glad he found my camera," Jamal said as he sat next to Asha. "Look, I can show you the picture we were talking about before."

"Oh yeah, I took a peek and saw it," Asha said as Jamal clicked through the photos.

"You did?" Jamal asked.

"Yeah, it's a wonderful picture. It's nearly unbelievable because it's my face in the sky," Asha replied.

"But why ... I mean, how do you think that happened? This can't all be some big coincidence, right?" Jamal asked.

Asha thought, "I can't tell him what I really think. We've only known each other for two days. If I tell him that I think my ancestors chose him to be my prince, it could petrify him." She finally replied, "I don't know, this is still a mystery to me, Jamal," laying her head on his chest. "I just want to enjoy this last night with you looking at the stars, okay?"

Jamal put his arm around her. "Me too." He wanted to kiss her, but was too shy to try it. At that moment, Jamal and Asha fell completely in love with each other. They silently stared at the stars until they fell asleep in each other's arms.

CHAPTER NINE

GOING AWAY

The next morning, King Juma knocked on Asha's door. "Asha!" he called, but as he continued to knock, no one answered. He then opened the door and saw that she was not in the main part of her room. He also noticed that the attic door was opened like it had been the night before. After climbing up the ladder into the attic, he spotted Jamal sleeping near Asha and Tamir sleeping near Halima on the floor. King Juma realized that Miss Enu had been right all along. He did not recognize Jamal or Tamir at all, and became infuriated. "Asha!" he yelled. Everyone in the attic immediately woke up. "What is this? Who are these guys?"

"Father, I can explain," Asha said, panicking.

King Juma did not allow Asha to explain herself. "Too late—your time is up! I'm calling the guards!" he shouted as he walked away, preparing to climb out of the attic. Asha ran after her father and grabbed his arm. "No, wait, Father, just listen!" she shouted.

"What is it?" King Juma asked fiercely.

"Two days ago, Halima and I found them near the river when their kayak got washed up on shore. They were lost and scared, and we came to their aid," she explained.

Jamal felt guilty, so he intervened in their conversation. "Yes, sorry about this, sir; this is all my fault. We fell into the river when I tried to get a picture of your kingdom. Your daughter and Halima saved us, and we really didn't mean to cause any harm."

King Juma placed his hand on his forehead, and his face took on a very confused look. "Wait, so the animals did not kill you?" he asked, clueless.

Asha frowned. "No, Father, they obviously didn't kill them if they're standing right here in front of you."

"Hmm...all of you meet me by the front door immediately," King Juma said as he climbed down the ladder, leaving the attic. Scared of what might happen next, Tamir and Jamal's hands began to tremble as they collected all of their belongings. "I'm really sorry about all of this, Asha," Jamal told her.

Asha gave Jamal a tight hug. "No, it's not your fault, Jamal; you're fine—I'll fix this, I promise."

While King Juma walked around the palace hallways, Queen Naomi caught up with him. "Juma, what's wrong? I heard you yelling," she said. Chancellor Hakim and Lady Iman came up behind them and asked what had happened. King Juma stopped walking for a moment to answer them. "Our daughters have snuck two strangers into the kingdom. I don't think they know how much danger they could have...or probably have put us in. Who knows what these guys are capable of?" King Juma said, still furious.

Queen Naomi wrapped her arms around the king's arm, trying to calm him down. "I'm sure Asha and Halima had a reason for doing what they did," she said gently.

Lady Iman chimed in as well to ease the tension. "Yes, maybe the boys were in trouble and needed help," she said.

"But they should've told us when this happened—then we wouldn't be in this situation," Chancellor Hakim told Lady Iman.

Moments later, Jamal, Tamir, Asha, and Halima met everyone at the front door. Jamal courageously approached the king and queen. "King Juma and Queen Naomi, I would like to apologize again for all of the trouble I caused," he said. King Juma's face showed no sign of emotion. He just firmly placed his right hand on Jamal's shoulder and said, "That's all right, my boy. Chancellor Hakim and I would like to speak to you and your friend outside." As King Juma opened the door, Asha grew worried. "We should go with them," she whispered to Halima.

Right then, Queen Naomi called to her and Halima. "Come here, girls—Iman and I will speak with you two in the living room."

Meanwhile, outside, King Juma and Chancellor Hakim were questioning Jamal and Tamir. "So, you two had no intentions of harming our kingdom or revealing any secrets?" Chancellor Hakim asked.

"No, sir, we did not. We won't even tell people that we've been inside of here," Tamir replied.

"That's right, sir," Jamal chimed in, "I wouldn't do

anything to expose the kingdom. I really care about your daughter, and I would love to keep in touch with her, I—"

"Care about her—keep in touch with her!" King Juma shouted. "Oh, no, son, you will not be keeping in touch with her. Ya see, she is about to get married soon to a great royal man named Yoba next week, and if you care about her, you will go now and never come back. We don't need strangers here disrupting our royal traditions."

Jamal looked surprised. I didn't know she was getting married next week, he thought to himself.

"Yes, and my Halima will be getting married the day after Asha's wedding," Chancellor Hakim said.

Let me guess—she's getting married to Namdi, right? Tamir thought, feeling a little distraught. Then the guards approached Jamal and Tamir, grabbing their arms. King Juma pointed toward the kingdom's front gates. "Look over there," he said. When Jamal and Tamir looked, they saw Mr. Kwame waving at them with a smile on his face. "I contacted the resort and talked to Mr. Kwame. He told me that you two were good kids and that you probably didn't mean any harm by coming here. So, I'm being lenient by having the guards escort you out to Mr. Kwame. You two really do seem like decent people, so do yourselves a favor: Go back home and live your lives. That way things are less complicated." The guards began escorting them out of the kingdom. Though Tamir and Jamal tried to resist a bit because they wanted to say their final goodbyes, they couldn't because the guards were too strong and there were too many of them. "Hey, boys, it looks like you guys caused quite the stir today," Mr. Kwame said, laughing, as the guards let go of Jamal and Tamir right outside of the kingdom.

"Yeah, I guess so," Tamir said as he dusted himself off.

"We didn't even have a chance to tell the girls goodbye," Jamal said.

"Aww, it's okay; you might see the girls again." Mr. Kwame said.

"Yeah right," Tamir replied in disbelief.

"Hey, kid ya never know how the universe may work," Mr. Kwame answered.

Moments later, Mr. Kwame took them to a helicopter waiting nearby that would take them back to the resort. "You're a pilot too?" Jamal asked.

"Yup, I do a little bit of everything," Mr. Kwame answered. As they sat in the helicopter, Mr. Kwame looked like he had many questions on his mind. "If you don't mind me asking, how did you two manage to get all the way down here?" he asked.

"Well, we went kayaking again to get a good picture of the kingdom. And remember when you said the boulder couldn't move?" Jamal asked.

"Yes," Mr. Kwame answered.

"Well, it moved...and when it moved, we fell straight down the waterfall," Jamal explained.

Mr. Kwame scratched his head. "And the animals didn't try to kill you?" he asked.

"Nope...well, the princess said that the animals just tried to frighten us a bit, that's all," Jamal replied.

"Wow!" Mr. Kwame said, a surprised look on his face. After taking the guys to get their things at the resort, Mr. Kwame dropped them off at the Matana airport and said, "Remember, boys, watch how the universe works."

"Mr. Kwame is crazy to think that somehow we will see them again," Tamir said as he and Jamal boarded the plane.

Meanwhile, back at the kingdom, Queen Naomi and Lady Iman talked with Asha and Halima. "Asha, how did this all start? Tell me everything," Queen Naomi said as she tried to get a full understanding of the entire situation.

"Well, Jamal and Tamir won a trip to the Matana resort by winning some art contest in their hometown. And the picture they took that won the contest for them had my face in the sky."

"Your face?" Queen Naomi cut in.

"Yes, Mother—they couldn't really explain it; it was like magic or something," Asha said. "When they got to the resort, they participated in the tour," she continued. "After that tour, they came back to the Matana River to get a good picture of our kingdom, but the big boulder that's slightly above the waterfall had moved."

"No way! That boulder has to weigh a ton," Lady Iman said, astonished by Asha's story.

"Yes, Mother, the boulder moved and they fell down the waterfall into the sea and washed up along shore," Halima told her.

"And the animals didn't kill them?" Queen Naomi and Lady Iman asked at the same time.

"No!" Asha and Halima answered at the same time. Queen Naomi and Lady Iman were speechless. "They even told us that the picture they took is hanging up in the lobby at the Matana resort," Halima said.

"That's right! Mother, they're wonderful guys, and me meeting Jamal can't be one big coincidence. There has to be a reason behind this, right?" Asha asked, trying to convince her mother that her ancestors had chosen Jamal as her prince.

"I...I guess so, sweetheart, if you feel that way. I'm so confused now, I don't know if your ancestors chose Yoba or if they chose Jamal. Oh, this is not good; how are we supposed to fulfill the prophecy now? The five-hundredth-year anniversary of the Battle of Matana is soon, Asha!" Queen Naomi said, panicking. "Asha, I need you to give me direct answers to the questions I'm about to ask you, okay?" she added, calming herself down.

"Okay, Mother," Asha replied.

"Do you love Yoba?" Queen Naomi asked.

"No!" Asha replied with a straight face.

"All right now, I know it's only been a few days that you've known Jamal, but do you love him?" Queen Naomi asked.

After a slight pause, Asha answered, "Yes, Mother, I love him with all my heart."

King Juma and Chancellor Hakim walked into the palace and came into the living room where everyone was talking. Asha got up from the couch and ran into the hall. "Jamal...Jamal," she said, looking into the hall and through the front door. "Father, where is Jamal?" she asked.

"Well, he thought it was best for him and Tamir to leave right away. He said congratulations on the marriage and have a nice life," King Juma answered.

Asha became teary-eyed. "He didn't even say goodbye," she said to herself as she ran to her room.

"I'll go after her," Halima said, chasing after Asha.

Queen Naomi was furious. "Why would you tell her that?" she asked.

"Honey, I want our daughter to be happy just as much as you do, but I have to do what I can to save our kingdom. She will be very happy soon, anyway...because if she doesn't marry Yoba, we will all die," King Juma replied sarcastically.

"Should we tell our husbands about the picture?" Lady Iman asked Queen Naomi when they were alone.

"Oh no, with the anniversary coming up, they are going to be too stubborn to hear anything we have to say about any of this. But don't worry; I have a plan," Queen Naomi said.

Meanwhile, upstairs in Asha's room, Halima was trying to calm her down. "Asha, relax—do you think Jamal would honestly say that?" she asked.

"I don't know; it depends on what my father told him," Asha answered.

"Well, I refuse to believe that they would just up and leave like that without saying anything to us," Halima said, trying to cheer Asha up.

"Yeah, you're right. I just wanted to see him one last time. Now I just want to stay locked away in my room forever," Asha said, burying her face in her pillow.
Queen Naomi and Lady Iman came into the room then. "Is everything okay now?" Lady Iman asked.

"No, Mother; Asha is devastated," Halima replied. "Queen Naomi, we must go to the resort so I can show you the picture. Asha, you stay here," she added.

As King Juma was approaching the door, Queen Naomi stepped out of the room and shut it.

"Well, can I talk to her?" King Juma asked.

"No! Not right now, anyway; she's going to stay in her room until the wedding. She said she is willing to uphold the tradition for her ancestors and that she wants Matana to be protected, so you can see her on the day of the wedding," Queen Naomi explained to King Juma, hoping he would believe her.

King Juma was so delusional that he bought it. "Ah...I

knew she would finally come around. I just want her to know that I mean no harm and that I'm just doing what's best for her and the kingdom," he said.

"Yes, I know, honey; I'll be sure to tell her that. She will be fine, and so will Matana," Queen Naomi said, kissing King Juma. Moments later, while King Juma and Chancellor Hakim went back to work, Queen Naomi, Lady Iman, and Halima rode in a royal carriage pulled by elephants and escorted by the guards all the way to the resort.

After hours and hours on the plane ride back home, Jamal and Tamir were just looking forward to everything being normal again. "Man, maybe I was stupid to fall head over heels for a girl I barely even know. I should've just listened to you the first day and stayed at the resort instead of going to take another picture of that kingdom," Jamal said to Tamir.

"Well, you shouldn't beat yourself up about it, and I must admit, we did have fun there. But hey, I foolishly fell in love too," Tamir said.

"I just...I just wish I'd never met her; that's all. Then this wouldn't hurt so much inside," Jamal said.

Tamir agreed. "I'm with you on that, bro. Thank God we have a graduation in two days. I think that will help us move forward."

Back in Matana, when Queen Naomi, Lady Iman, and Halima arrived in the lobby at the Matana resort, everyone bowed down. "Your Highness," the people said to the queen as she walked around with her presence lighting up the entire lobby. "Hello everyone!" Queen Naomi said with a wide smile on her face. Halima then saw Asha's picture hanging up in the lobby. "Mother! Queen Naomi! Here it is!" she said as she ran to get a closer look at the picture.

"Wow, it's beautiful!" Lady Iman said.

Queen Naomi gasped. "The ancestors must've really chosen Jamal to be Asha's prince," she said as she touched the picture.

"Oh yeah, Queen Naomi, I must mention one more thing," Halima said.

"And what is that?" Queen Naomi asked.

"Yesterday, when Asha and Jamal were on the base of the Queen Asha statue, I believe I saw the statue's eyes glow. Before, I thought I was hallucinating, but now, I believe it really happened."

"Are you sure?" Lady Iman asked, approaching Halima.

"Yes, Mother, I'm sure."

"Okay, here's what I'm going to do. I'm going to send you and Asha to America to get Jamal and bring him back just in time for the wedding. During the wedding, when Yoba and Asha are on the step, everyone will notice that the statue's eyes are not glowing. Once that happens, Jamal will have to come out of his hiding spot and immediately get on the step to prove to everyone that our ancestors chose Asha as his soulmate," Queen Naomi explained cheerfully.

Later that night, when Queen Naomi, Lady Iman, and Halima returned to the palace, Halima ran upstairs into Asha's room. "Asha! I have great news—we're going to bring Jamal back. We're leaving first thing in the morning!" Halima said.

Asha instantly removed her blankets and sat up. "No way! Are you serious?" she said in shock.

"Yes, even your mother is fine with it," Halima replied.

At that moment, Queen Naomi came into Asha's room. "Hey, sweetie, I will keep your father distracted for the next few days while you and Halima are in America looking for Jamal. I'm allowing you to do this because I know that Jamal is truly your soulmate. I saw the picture, honey, and the ancestors have never made a mistake," she told Asha.

"Thank you, Mother; I love you so much," Asha said, hugging the queen.

"I love you too, sweetie. All right now, here's the money for you and Halima. Iman will escort both of you to the airport tomorrow morning. We also talked to Mr. Kwame at the resort, and he is willing to help sneak you two there without being noticed. So be safe, okay? I know the ancestors will protect you."

The following morning, Lady Iman hid the girls in the back of a green truck with tinted windows as Mr. Kwame drove them to the airport. "Hello, girls. So I see this is turning out to be quite the love story," he said.

The girls laughed. "Yes, I guess it is," Halima replied.

"Halima, do you have feelings for that Tamir fella?" Lady Iman asked curiously.

"Nah," Halima answered with no emotion.

Asha nudged Halima, smirking. "Yes, you do," Asha

revealed.

"Okay, you got me. Yes, I like him," Halima said.

"I knew I sensed something, but hey, it's okay if you do. This entire day has been eventful and surprising. And ya never know—maybe the ancestors chose him for you too," Lady Iman told Halima.

"Now before you two get on the plane, you have to change your clothes," Mr. Kwame said.

Asha looked concerned. "Change our clothes! Why?" she asked.

"Because you will no longer be in Matana; you will be in America, and they dress completely different over there," Lady Iman explained.

"Oh, okay, so what are we going to wear?" Asha asked. Lady Iman pulled out a big box from underneath her seat and said, "Your clothes are in here; you can change in the restroom in the back of the truck." The girls went and changed in the restroom. Asha put on a brown leather jacket with a black shirt and black pants, and Halima put on a black leather jacket with a blue shirt and tan pants. "All right, girls, you're going to follow me. We're taking my private jet," Mr. Kwame said.

"I didn't know you were a pilot too," Halima replied.

Mr. Kwame laughed, saying, "I'm a lot of things."

"Okay, girls, give me a hug," Lady Iman said, starting to cry. "You two are growing up so fast—I can't believe your marriages are right around the corner. All right, I'll let you girls go now. Be safe, okay?" she added as she hugged them both.

CHAPTER TEN

HOME SWEET HOME

Jamal and Tamir had landed at the airport in the city on the day that Asha and Halima entered the jet in Matana. At the airport, Jamal and Tamir were both greeted by their families. Maya and Aaliyah were extremely excited to see their brothers, running toward them and hugging them really tightly.

"Hey, guys! How was Matana?" Maya asked.

After Maya's question Aaliyah proceeded to bombard them with even more questions. "Yeah, was it fun? Did you see lions?"

Tamir and Jamal giggled. "Yes, it was fun, and yes, we did see lions," Tamir said.

"And we brought you girls something from the gift shop," Jamal added as he reached into his bag. "These are royal Matana princess dolls, so you have to treat them very special, okay?" He handed Maya and Aaliyah the dolls they'd bought.

"Wow, they're beautiful! Thank you, big bro," Maya gushed.

"Yeah, thanks for not forgetting about us," Aaliyah said playfully while hugging both Jamal and Tamir.

"Aw, it's cute that you two went out of your way to get something for your little sisters," Mrs. Sanders said sarcastically.

"We got gifts for the parents, too!" Tamir protested.

"I knew you wouldn't forget about your momma," Mrs. Sanders said with a grin.

The next morning Jamal and Tamir began to prepare for their graduation. They were happy about graduating, but a piece of them still wanted to be in Matana. As Jamal looked at his reflection in his bedroom mirror that morning, he began to talk to himself. "All right, Jamal, today is the day you graduate. I guess it's time to move forward with your life now and leave the past behind," he said as he put on his cap and gown.

After Tamir put on his cap and gown, he looked at the selfie he and Halima had taken on his phone. "Man, I really need to get over this girl," he told himself as he deleted the photo.

"Hey man, you ready to go?" Jamal asked Tamir as he came downstairs.

"Yeah bro, let's go... I'm driving," Tamir answered.

"All right, guys, we'll be right in the audience watching you two walk across that stage," Mrs. Howard said cheerfully.

"Okay, mom, see ya," Jamal replied.

After a long flight and finally landing at City Airport, Mr. Kwame gave the girls spare cell phones and told them that he would be close by and to call if they needed him. When they entered the city, Asha and Halima were irked by how everything was so busy, noisy, and close together. "This place is making my brain hurt," Halima complained.

"I know, and I have no idea how to work these cellphones that Mr. Kwame gave us," Asha told Halima.

"Oh, don't worry about that—Tamir showed me how to

operate these things a couple days ago," Halima explained.

"I think I even had his number written down in my..." She reached into all of her pockets. "Ugh, oh no! I left it back home,"

"Aw, no! Well, we have to figure out something," Asha said.

"I remember Tamir telling me about those yellow cars we see driving by right now. They're called um...taxis—yeah, taxis, that's right. All we have to do is pay them for a ride," Halima said.

"Okay, well, I see them driving on the road, but how do we get them to stop?" Asha asked as she walked closer to the curb. Suddenly a taxi pulled up on the side of the curb in front of them.

"Well, I guess that's how," Halima replied.

"Hey, do you fine ladies need a ride?" the taxi driver asked.

"Yes," Asha confirmed.

"So where ya headed?" the taxi driver asked once they'd climbed in.

"City University," Halima told him.

"Oh, okay, they're having a graduation today. Do you girls know someone that goes there?" the driver wondered as he began to drive.

"Yes, my husband is graduating today!" Asha said excitingly.

"Aw, so you're taken! What about you, sweet thing?" the man asked Halima.

"Yes, I'm taken, too! My husband is graduating as well," Halima quickly told the driver.

"All right, well, we're here—and congrats to your loved ones!" the driver said.

"Thank you. Here's the money," Asha said as she gave the driver a decent-size amount of cash.

The driver's eyes widened as he took the cash. "Wow! Thanks for the tip, baby. Hey, if it doesn't work out with your husbands, I'm always available." He smiled and showed some of his missing teeth before driving off.

As Asha and Halima entered the University, the staff led them to the auditorium and helped them sit in the last row to watch the graduation ceremony.

During the graduation ceremony, Jamal and Tamir were in line preparing to have their names called to receive their degrees. After waiting and waiting, Jamal was finally next to walk across the stage. "Up next, with a degree in Marketing, we have Jamal Howard," the Dean said as she read the teleprompter.

As Jamal walked across the stage and grabbed his degree, the crowd cheered and applauded. When the cheering died down, he heard someone in the back scream, "GO JAMAL!" He thought he recognized the voice, but he couldn't see who it was because the lights from the stage were beaming in his face; so, after looking, he continued to walk across the stage.

As his family turned back to see who had yelled, Asha and Halima crouched down in their seats. "I'm just going to keep quiet for now," Asha whispered in embarrassment. "I'll do the same, girl," Halima replied while snickering.

After everyone had received their degrees and was waiting for the ceremony to end, Tamir tried to get Jamal's attention by waving at him. "What's up?" Jamal whispered to Tamir.

"Did the voice that screamed your name sound like Asha to you?" Tamir asked.

"Shush!" a woman who was sitting behind Tamir said. Jamal began to think about the voice; it really had sounded like Asha.

When the graduation ceremony ended, Jamal and Tamir met up with their families. "We're so proud of you guys," Mrs. Howard said as she and Mr. Howard took turns hugging them.

Seconds later, Mr. Sanders and Mrs. Sanders ran up to Jamal and Tamir, hugging them and lifting them up in excitement. "Congratulations, guys!" Mr. Sanders said excitedly.

"I know you guys are ready for your Graduation Cookout," Mrs. Sanders added.

"We sure are," Tamir replied happily.

"Yeah, I'm starving," Jamal said.

"All right, we'll see you there soon," Mrs. Howard said as they all began to walk outside.

"Oh no, they're leaving! We have to catch up to them," Asha told Halima hurriedly.

"Don't worry, we will! I just have to pee really bad, girl. I'm just going to the ladies' room. I'll be right back," Halima told her while rushing to the restroom.

As Asha waited outside the restroom for Halima, she peeked through the crowd and saw Jamal and Tamir talking to each other right outside the door. While panicking and thinking that they would walk away, Asha began to run out toward the building to catch up to Jamal.

"Hey bro, I have to go to the bathroom really quick. I'll be right back," Tamir told Jamal as they headed to their car.

Suddenly, Maya hopped out of Mr. Howard's car and handed Jamal a card that said 'Congratulations Graduate' on it. "Sorry, big bro, I forgot to give this to you before we left," she said.

"Thanks, Maya," Jamal replied with a grin.

"Hey, who were those two girls that were here to see you? One of them screamed your name," Maya wondered.

"I have no clue. I couldn't see them. What did they look like?" Jamal asked.

"One girl was dark-skinned with pretty long dreads..."

"Maya, come on, we have to get ready for the cookout!" Mr. Howard shouted from the car, cutting off Maya's description.

"And the other girl was light-skinned with a pretty afro," Maya finished as she ran back to Mr. and Mrs. Howard's car.

Jamal quickly took off running back toward the University, ignoring the fact that it suddenly began to rain heavily. As he got close to the building's door, he spotted Asha coming outside looking for him. "JAMAL!" Asha yelled.

Jamal didn't say a word; he was once again captivated by Asha's beauty. At that moment, Jamal walked up to her and kissed her in the pouring rain while he still had his cap and gown on. For Jamal, it was like time had suddenly slowed down. He couldn't even feel or hear the raindrops splashing onto their faces. It was as if they were suspended between time and space.

After they finished kissing, Jamal said, "Would it be weird if I told you that I love you? I mean, I know I've only known you for a few days, but…"

"Shush!" Asha said as she placed her finger on Jamal's

lips. "I love you too," she whispered, following the confession with another kiss.

"And I want you to know that I didn't choose to leave. I wanted to at least say goodbye first, but the guards carried us out," Jamal explained.

"Oh, don't worry about that. I know my father was the one who got you kicked out. I'm just happy to see you again," Asha reassured him.

Meanwhile, back inside the university, Tamir and Halima were walking out of the restrooms at the same time. Tamir left the men's room looking down and wiping his hands, and Halima walked out of the women's restroom fixing her hair.

"Tamir!" Halima exclaimed as their eyes met.

"Hey Ha—"

Before Tamir could even complete his sentence, Halima grabbed him by the face and gave him a quick kiss.

"Woah! Well, that greeting was better than our first one... What are you doing here?" Tamir asked.

"We came to see you graduate!" Halima said sarcastically.

Tamir gave her a knowing smirk. "And?"

"And we came to bring you and Jamal back to Matana, because Jamal will be Asha's prince!" Halima rapidly explained in excitement.

"For real? Come on, I have to take you two to see Jamal," Tamir said while grabbing Halima by the arm and running outside.

"Where the heck is Asha?" Halima thought to herself as she went with Tamir.

"Hey Jamal, look who I found!" Tamir shouted as he and Halima spotted Jamal.

"Hey, Halima!" Jamal said. "Yeah, I ran into Asha out here."

"Hey, Asha! You girls should come to our graduation cookout! You'll love it," Tamir said.

"Okay," Asha replied.

"You're going to love the food, Halima. We're going to have mac and cheese, pasta salad, green beans, corn on the cob, fried chicken, burgers, hot dogs, and fried fish," Tamir explained enthusiastically.

"No fruit?" Halima wondered.

"Oh yeah, we'll have fruit too," Tamir assured her.

At the cookout, Jamal and Tamir introduced Asha and Halima to their families, including their parents, grandparents, aunts, uncles, and cousins.

"So, Jamal and Tamir, where did you meet these two lovely ladies?" Mrs. Sanders asked.

Jamal and Tamir couldn't think about what to say when it came to answering that question. "Um," Jamal said as he tapped his chin.

"Ah," Tamir said, looking clueless.

Asha immediately chimed in. "We met them in Matana. We showed them many of our landmarks and what life is like over there, and now they're returning the favor by showing us what life is like in the city," she explained.

Mrs. Howard smiled. "That's great! I'd noticed you ladies had an accent, so that's where you're from—Matana, Africa?"

"Yes, ma'am," Halima confirmed.

"So how are you two liking the city so far?" Mrs. Howard asked.

"It's nice so far, although it's a lot noisier and busier here, but we learned how to catch a cab today... That was interesting," Asha offered.

"Oh yes, the city can be a bit much sometimes, but you know what? You girls will probably love the street mall. Mrs. Sanders and I used to take the subway every weekend and go to the mall as teens."

Cutting off his mom before she got deep into her story, Jamal said, "Okay, mom, we'll take them to the mall after we eat!"

"TIME TO EAT!" Mr. Sanders suddenly shouted.

Tamir quickly grabbed Halima's hand and ran to the food, making her a plate with all of the dishes he'd mentioned before. "Wait , wait, wait," Halima protested while laughing.

"What's wrong?" Tamir demanded.

"I can't eat all of this by myself!" she replied.

Tamir snickered. "Oh, don't worry I'm going to eat it with you. We can share this one big plate."

"Thank God!" she replied with a big smile on her face.

As Jamal and Asha patiently waited in line for the food, he could sense that there was more that Asha wanted to tell him, but maybe she didn't feel comfortable.

"Do you want to share a plate too?" Jamal asked jokingly.

"Sure, I don't see why not," Asha said as she held his hand.

"I don't eat as much as Tamir, so my plate is going to look like a smaller portion of his," Jamal told her.

"That's fine—I don't eat as much as Halima either."

"All right, Tamir, you got me…the food was amazing. It even gave Matana's food a run for its money," Halima said after finishing up their plate.

"I knew you would love it," Tamir said presumptuously.

Later on, Maya and Aaliyah approached Asha and Halima. "This is my little sister Maya and Tamir's little sister Aaliyah," Jamal explained.

"You two are really pretty," Maya told them.

"Thank you!" Asha and Halima replied at the same time. "You two are pretty too," Asha added.

"Thank you! I love your jewelry. Is that from Matana too?" Aaliyah asked.

"Yes, it is from Matana. Asha and I actually have gold necklaces that you can have," Halima told the girls.

"Really?" Maya asked excitingly.

"Yeah, here ya go," Asha said as she and Halima placed small gold necklaces around the girls' necks.

After enjoying the cookout, Jamal and Tamir drove Asha and Halima through the city with the top down in the car. Asha and Halima gazed at the city lights while the night wind blew through their hair. It didn't matter if it was street lights, building lights, traffic lights, or the headlights on cars: it all looked beautiful to them.

"Before we leave the city, we're going to take you two to the street mall to try some cinnamon pretzels and show you around," Jamal said.

"Pretzels... What are those?" Halima asked.

"It's just baked dough twisted in a knot; we're going to have cinnamon added to it. You'll love it, I promise," Tamir explained.

While they were at the street mall, they ordered cinnamon pretzels and took a walk around the streets. "I love the pretzels, Tamir. I guess the food here in America isn't so bad after all," Halima told him as they walked together with their arms around each other.

"I agree with her—these pretzels are to die for!" Asha said as she bit into hers and savored the taste. "The city is such a beautiful place at night. I just don't know how you deal with all of this noise," she added.

"Well, when I want to get away from all the noise, I usually go to this spot called City Hill. It's located right on the outskirts of the city," Jamal explained.

"Wow, can I see it?" Asha asked.

"Sure," Jamal answered. "Yo Tamir, I'll be back—I'm going to show Asha where City Hill is!" he shouted as he took the car.

"All right, bro," Tamir replied while he and Halima stayed at the street mall.

After driving up to City Hill, Jamal told Asha to close her eyes. While helping her step out of the car, he even placed his hands over her eyes just in case she peeked. "Just listen to my voice and take one step at a time," he told her as they got closer to the view.

"All right, now open your eyes," Jamal whispered. Asha opened her eyes, and the scenery took her breath away. There were so many scattered lights surrounded by darkness. She loved the way the bridge lit up as the cars drove across it. And across the dark river, she could see buildings and streetlights that looked like big stars from miles away.

"I love it! This is beautiful!" Asha gasped with a smile on her face.

After enjoying the scenery, Asha felt that it was the perfect time to talk to Jamal about going back to Matana. "Jamal, we have to talk," she said seriously.

"Okay, what's up?" he asked.

"All right, I'm just going to be straightforward with him," Asha thought to herself. "Jamal," she explained, "my ancestors chose you to be my prince. I know this sounds crazy, but we have to get married in a couple days to save Matana."

Jamal looked bewildered. "Woah... They actually chose me to be your prince?" After processing this information, Jamal began to speak about what was on his mind. "I guess in the back of my mind I started to figure that out, but to actually hear you say it lets me know that this is real and that there's no turning back."

"How do you feel about this?" Asha asked.

"I feel rejuvenated and happy because you've changed my life. You make me happy, and I love you," Jamal said as he hugged Asha and gave her a quick kiss.

Asha was relieved to hear his response. "I love you too. Oh my God, I can't believe that you're actually okay with this. Are you going to tell your parents?"

"Oh no! Right now, it's just too soon, and I'd need to explain how this whole thing happened. My mom is going to kill me regardless," Jamal answered.

Asha laughed, "It's okay, I understand."

Suddenly Jamal began to wonder about the curse. "Hey Asha, do you think that this curse will still happen?" he asked.

"No, not at all. Now that I know you're my prince, it should no longer exist," Asha told Jamal.

"Okay, cool—but for some reason, it just won't leave my mind," he said.

"Don't worry. Before you know it, we'll be in Matana having a peaceful wedding," Asha reassured him.

"Wow, I can't believe I'm actually getting married tomorrow. Aw man, I just realized we have to book our plane tickets now," Jamal said eagerly.

"Uh, we actually have a private jet ready for us," Asha told him with a smile.

"Let me guess... Mr. Kwame is the pilot, right?" Jamal stated.

"Yup, you got it," Asha agreed.

That night, Jamal and Tamir told their parents that they were going on a road trip for a few days to celebrate their graduation, even though they were really traveling back to Matana.

CHAPTER ELEVEN

THE ROYAL SURPRISE

At midnight, Jamal and Asha picked Tamir and Halima up at the mall and drove them to the airport to meet Mr. Kwame. As they boarded the jet, Mr. Kwame said, "Hey, guys, I told you the universe would pull it off. It never fails. Now you kids get some rest. We have a long flight ahead of us."

"Good. In a minute I'll be out like a log," Tamir said as he yawned and leaned his chair back.

After a long flight and a good sleep, they reached Matana in the afternoon. Mr. Kwame contacted Queen Naomi and Lady Iman to let them know the princess was back. Queen Naomi and Lady Iman met up with them, and they snuck Jamal and Tamir into the kingdom by hiding them in the zebra-drawn royal carriage. After they entered the palace, Queen Naomi and Lady Iman made sure no one was around and then found wedding outfits for Jamal, Asha, Tamir, and Halima to wear during the ceremony.

"Jamal and Tamir, come with me. I'll get you dressed," Lady Iman said.

"Asha and Halima, you two come with me. I will get you dressed," Queen Naomi instructed.

Jamal and Tamir thought it was funny that Lady Iman was getting them dressed. She put their shirts on them, tightened their pants, and set a crown on Jamal's head.

"Man, I feel like a little kid getting dressed by my momma," Jamal giggled.

"Oh, but you are such a strapping young man. Both of you are," Lady Iman told them. She squeezed their cheeks as if they were babies. "Now let's get you back into the royal carriage until the wedding starts. Did Asha explain the plan to you?"

"Yup. I'm going to come out when the king sees that the statue doesn't light up for Yoba," Jamal answered.

"Correct," Lady Iman said.

As the girls finished dressing, Queen Naomi began to cry. "Sweetheart, you look so beautiful! I can't believe your day is finally here!" she said, hugging Asha.

"I'm just as happy as you are, mother. Thank you for letting me marry my soulmate," Asha said, wiping tears from her own face.

Later, Lady Iman rode the carriage to the wedding ceremony. A long, wide floor had risen suddenly from under the sea and now stretched from the base of the statue of Queen Asha all the way across the land. This helped the citizens gather around the statue to watch the wedding. Lady Iman steered close to the statue so Jamal and Tamir could get a better look. A few seconds later, they saw children walking down the aisle scattering rose petals while other children played drums.

"The wedding is beginning!" a preacher announced as he walked up to the base of the statue.

Moments later, Halima walked down the aisle, being the maid of honor, and was followed by Namdi, Yoba's best man. Yoba followed with his parents and his grandmother Miss Enu escorting him. Then two royal guards blew rams' horns to signal that the king, queen, and princess were coming. The entire kingdom grew so quiet you could hear a leaf hit the ground. Finally, King Juma, Queen Naomi, and Princess Asha began to walk slowly down the aisle.

"She is the most beautiful woman in the world. I can't wait for her to be my wife," Jamal thought as he watched from inside the carriage.

As Asha approached Yoba, King Juma and Queen Naomi gave her a hug and took seats among the crowd. Yoba reached out to take her hand, and they both stepped onto the base of the statue. King Juma wore a huge grin as he watched them. Asha looked at the statue's eyes, hoping they wouldn't glow.

After an entire minute, the statue's eyes still were not glowing. The citizens grew concerned, and King Juma's grin faded. "What's going on? Why isn't it glowing?" he asked.

Miss Enu grew worried. "This can't be happening right now. Today is the anniversary of the battle," she said, pulling on her hair.

"Go ahead, Bro, it's your time now," Tamir told Jamal.

Jamal jumped out of the carriage, and at that moment a bolt of lightning struck the spirit energy ball hovering above the statue's hand and extinguished it. The sky started turning a deep red. "Aw shoot, I'm too late," Jamal said quietly to himself.

The crowd grew wary as bloodshot clouds spread over the kingdom. "The curse! It's happening!" King Juma shouted. Everyone started running, scared for their lives and trying to find places to hide.

"Okay, you know what? I didn't sign up for this. Maybe I'm unfit for this position," Yoba said. He hopped off the statue and ran down the aisle to hide with everyone else.

"What are we going to do, Juma?" Chancellor Hakim

asked.

"JAMAL HAS TO MARRY ASHA!" Queen Naomi shouted.

"O—" As King Juma tried to shout "okay," he was struck and killed by a bolt of lightning.

The people of Matana screamed as a swarm of demonic figures flew about, striking people with lightning bolts that killed them on impact. The demons wore black cloaks and had pale skin, sharp teeth, and piercing red eyes.

"FATHER!" Asha screamed when she saw her mother crying over his lifeless body. Asha was in shock and couldn't move. Her heart pounded rapidly, and she feared for her life.

Seeing Asha standing terrified and alone near the statue, Jamal ran as fast as he could against the flow of the crowd. "ASHA! WAIT RIGHT THERE! HERE I COME!" he shouted.

While Queen Naomi, Lady Iman, and Chancellor Hakim tried to revive King Juma, a demon came upon them from behind and blasted them with a huge lightning bolt, killing all three.

By this time, in the middle of the chaos, Tamir was out of the carriage and running around trying to find Halima in the crowd. But when he finally spotted her, she was already on the ground lifeless. Realizing that there was nothing he could do, he dropped to his knees and started crying. "NO!" he shouted, with tears streaming down his face. As Tamir held onto Halima, he too was struck down by one of the demons.

Citizens, guards, and animals began to die left and right as the demons attacked them. Asad, Afia, Dayo, Nailah, Jojo and the rest of the animals fought back, but the demons were too powerful.

As Jamal finally reached the statue, the weather became stormy, and the wind grew wickedly strong. Jamal seized the statue and Asha as tightly as he could so that she wouldn't blow away. "Stay with me! Okay, I know there's a way to fix this!" he explained, holding Asha in his arms as she cried.

As Asha lifted her head from Jamal's chest and looked around, she saw her father, mother, Halima, Tamir, Lady Iman, Chancellor Hakim, Zane, her pets, and the rest of the royal citizens lying dead on the ground. "But they're all dead! Everyone's dead, Jamal!" she said with fear as she continued to sob.

Jamal stayed strong for Asha. "I know everyone's dead, but—" he stopped mid-sentence and looked up at the statue. Its eyes were glowing.

"Look, Asha! You see that? The eyes are glowing! That means your ancestors are with you. And I'm with you! Remember that Asha, you told me that. The power is in you! The power has always been in you! It was your face that I saw in the sky, you're the one who saved me, you're the one who gave me a chance! You're the one who let me into your kingdom when no one else would, and you're the one I fell in love with! I'm going to fight by your side every step of the way." Jamal explained emotionally as the rain and wind picked up even more.

Asha wiped tears off her face and stood up. "Okay . . . okay, I can do this," she whispered as she watched the demons beginning to surround her and Jamal. She closed her eyes and put her hands together in a prayer formation. "Dear ancestors, I need you more than ever now. I pray for your spirits to protect and guide me through this battle. I am one with you, and you are one with me."

She grabbed Jamal's hands just as the spirit energy from the statue came back and flew into them. Their eyes turned to gold, and golden fire began to emanate from their hands. They flew from the ground and began striking down demons with the gold fire coming from their palms. Every demon they hit burned away, turned into black smoke, and evaporated from their presence.

Suddenly, two demons grabbed Jamal from behind and shocked him with their lightning bolts. One shouted to Asha, "I WILL TORTURE YOU LIKE I TORTURED YOUR ANCESTORS 500 YEARS AGO!"

At that moment, Asha knew who the demons were. As she stared at Jamal where he laid on the ground, not knowing whether he was dead or alive, she became furious. "I'VE HAD ENOUGH OF THIS! I'M SENDING YOU TO HELL, WHERE YOU BELONG, ZIMMER AND ZELDA!" She felt the spirit of Queen Asha and thrust her arms powerfully forward, sending out a huge blast of fire. It evaporated Zimmer and Zelda, along with the rest of the demons.

Afterward, Asha was on her knees catching her breath. Her eye color returned to normal, and Jamal suddenly woke up. "Oh my God, you're alive!" Asha said joyfully, hugging him.

"And you're alive too! It's good to see you again," Jamal replied.

CHAPTER TWELVE

A NEW LIFE

Asha's ancestors King Yoba and Queen Asha came down to them in spirit form. "We are proud of you, Asha. You're truly going to make a great queen," Queen Asha told her as they hugged.

"Thank you, ancestor," Asha replied gratefully.

"And you're truly going to make a great king," King Yoba told Jamal while embracing him as well.

"Thank you, King Yoba. So is the curse finally gone?" Jamal asked.

"Yes, the curse is gone forever now," King Yoba replied.

Queen Asha walked over to Jamal and Asha and placed their hands together. "Take care of each other and set a great example for the future generations of kings and queens to come. Goodbye, my loves, and remember to show the people that the power of the ancestors is within them," the ancestral queen said as she and King Yoba faded away.

As they disappeared, the sky transitioned from red back to blue. Quickly restored, Matana began to look like a rich and beautiful kingdom again, with all of its citizens and animals coming back to life.

When Halima woke up, she spotted Tamir lying near her feet. "Tamir," she said frantically as she nudged him. "Wake up, oh my God, please wake up!" She started to shake him even harder.

When Tamir woke up, he sat up and looked Halima in her eyes. "You're alive, you're really alive," he gasped.

"And so are you!" Halima replied excitingly.

Tamir quickly kissed her. "I want to marry you. Do you want to marry me? Because I want to marry you."

"Yes, I do," Halima answered with a big smile on her face. "But let's plan and prepare for it because I want my wedding to look as beautiful as this one," she added as she looked around at how Asha's wedding was set up.

After waking up, Queen Naomi and King Juma raced over to Asha and hugged her really tight. "Oh my God, sweetheart, are you okay?" Queen Naomi asked.

"Yes mother, I'm fine! Jamal helped me defeat those evil bastards, and we finally put an end to the curse," Asha said.

"You hear that, Juma? They saved us. Jamal was Asha's soulmate all along!" Chancellor Hakim exclaimed.

King Juma walked up to Jamal with an emotionless face. "I want to apologize for giving you a rough time before, young man," he said, and then he smiled and hugged Jamal, lifting him off the ground. "BUT I WANT TO THANK YOU FOR FALLING IN LOVE WITH MY DAUGHTER!"

As the citizens cheered, King Juma put Jamal down and restarted the royal wedding, but this time with Jamal as the prince.

As Jamal walked to the base of the statue, Tamir ran to him and asked, "I can be your best man, right?"

"Oh yeah—of course, bro. Come up here," Jamal replied

happily.

"I hope you can be my best man too," Tamir whispered.

Jamal looked surprised. "You and Halima?" he questioned.

"Yup," Tamir replied.

"Already?" Jamal asked sarcastically.

"Soon," Tamir agreed.

"That's great, man. I'm happy for you two," Jamal said.

Their conversation was interrupted when Asha came walking down the aisle with a beautiful smile on her face as she looked at Jamal. As she made it to the base of the statue, the statue's eyes lit up, and the spirit energy hovering above the statue's hand grew brighter. "I'm ready to be your king." Jamal told Asha as he took her by the hand.

"And I'm ready to be your queen." Asha told him in return.

Suddenly, a new minister came racing down the aisle. "Sorry I'm late! I was on my tour guiding duties," the minister panted.

Jamal noticed that it was Mr. Kwame. "Mr. Kwame!" he said in shock.

"It's Minister Kwame today, young man," Mr. Kwame replied cheerfully.

"I contacted him and told him he should be the one to marry you two," Lady Iman said.

"That old man truly is a jack of all trades," Queen Naomi added.

Minister Kwame opened his sacred book and looked toward Jamal to ask, "Do you love her?"

"Yes," Jamal answered immediately.

Minister Kwame then looked at Asha and asked, "Do you love him?"

"Yes," Asha answered.

"All right then, you are now husband and wife and soon to be King and Queen of Matana! You may now kiss the princess," Minister Kwame exclaimed.

As Jamal and Asha kissed, the royal citizens and animals of Matana celebrated. "I'm so happy for you two! I don't think we have to train you on how to protect this kingdom because you both already have the power," King Juma said excitedly.

"Jamal, do you plan on living here in Matana?" Queen Naomi asked.

"Yeah, I..." Jamal began.

Asha cut him off. "We plan on going back and forth to stay in his hometown sometimes, but we're going to stay here at the kingdom sometimes, too," she said.

"King Juma and Queen Naomi, I think you would love meeting my family in the City. You should come visit them with us," Jamal offered.

"Oh yes, you really are going to love his family. They're really nice people," Asha said.

"And the food in America is surprisingly good," Halima told them.

"Wait—how do you two know his family?" King Juma

asked.

"Yes, how?" Chancellor Hakim demanded.

Queen Naomi and Lady Iman rolled their eyes, annoyed by their husbands' questions. "We'll explain that to you later," Queen Naomi told them.

All of a sudden, Zane, who'd been eavesdropping on their conversation, began to tug on Queen Naomi's dress to get her attention. "Can I visit America with you?" he asked.

"Zane, I have to see if that's okay with your mother and father," Queen Naomi told him.

"If I'm with the King and Queen, they wouldn't care," Zane assured her.

Queen Naomi started laughing at Zane's comment. "Come on, let's go see," she said as they went to go ask his parents.

The next day, they all arrived in the City with tons of security. The people in the City became so curious about why there was so much security around these people that they began to take pictures of the King, Queen, Chancellor, Lady Iman, and Zane, since they were still dressed in their royal uniforms.

Tamir had arranged for his parents to meet up at Jamal's condo. After taking the visitors from Matana to the condo, Jamal and Tamir introduced their parents to Asha and Halima's parents, and Zane got a chance to meet Maya and Aaliyah.

Jamal's parents were astonished. "Did you say Asha's parents are a King and Queen? That explains the royal clothing," Mr. Howard said.

"Yeah, Dad, they live in a kingdom, and Asha is a princess," Jamal explained.

"Oh my God, that is wonderful! Well, it's a pleasure to meet you, King Juma and Queen Naomi; your daughter is a sweetie pie," Mrs. Howard said.

"It's nice to meet you too, and thank you!" the King and Queen said at the same time.

"Mom and Dad, these are Halima's parents, Chancellor Hakim and Lady Iman," Tamir offered.

"Hello. I had the pleasure of getting to know your daughter the last time she was here," Mrs. Sanders said.

"And we had a great time getting to know your son," Lady Iman told Tamir's parents.

"Well, it looks like they're getting along well," Zane told Maya and Aaliyah as they sat on the couch.

"Yeah, your family seems cool...and rich!" Aaliyah answered.

"I'm just a family friend; Asha and Halima are like big sisters to me," Zane explained.

Changing the subject, Maya quickly grabbed a shoebox that was near her foot and said, "Hey Zane, do you want to see our pet hamsters?"

Zane looked confused. "Sure, but what are hamsters?"

"It's a rodent. They kind of look like mice without tails," Maya explained as she and Aaliyah pulled their hamsters out of the shoebox.

"This is Sunshine!" Aaliyah said.

"And this is Brownie," said Maya.

"Can I pet them?" Zane asked excitingly.

"Sure," Aaliyah answered. "Do you have any pets back home?"

"Yes, I have plenty of pets back home. I have a gorilla named Jojo, a cheetah named Nailah, and I also have hyenas, jaguars, and meerkats," Zane explained.

Maya's and Aaliyah's mouths dropped open. "Wow!" they said at the same time.

"We have to visit Matana soon," Maya told Aaliyah.

"Hey, everyone, I have an announcement to make!" Tamir said, getting everyone's attention. He then took a deep breath and said, "Halima and I are going to get married!"

Chancellor Hakim and Lady Iman jumped with joy. "That's great! We can have the wedding take place in

Matana again," Chancellor Hakim said.

This announcement completely caught Tamir's parents off-guard, however. Mrs. Sanders stood up. "Wait, what?" she asked. "Tamir, your father and I barely know Halima and her family. Don't get me wrong, you are all very nice people, but don't you feel like this is all being rushed?"

"No, not at all, Mom. I can explain everything to you, and that's why her parents are here—so you can all get to know each other. You have to trust my instinct on this," Tamir passionately explained to Mrs. Sanders.

"Okay...but you guys have to have a wedding in the City as well as Matana," Mrs. Sanders conceded.

"All right, Mom," Tamir agreed as he hugged her.

Mr. Sanders, thankfully, was a little more relaxed about the situation. "If you are all right with Halima and her family, then they're all right with me, son," he said.

"Thanks, Dad," Tamir answered sincerely.

"Hey, Chancellor Hakim, did you use the words 'wedding' and 'again' in the same sentence?" Mrs. Howard asked, curious about what the Chancellor had meant.

Jamal quickly intervened. "Uh—yes, Mom," he said while scratching his head. "Me and Asha are married now, and I'm a prince! And whenever King Juma and Queen Naomi are ready to step down, Asha and I will be the King and Queen of Matana," he explained.

Mrs. Howard nearly fainted, taking a deep breath and sitting down on the couch. She couldn't even think of anything to say.

Mr. Howard, on the other hand, smiled and hugged Jamal and Asha with joy. "Wow, my son is a prince! And hey, I'm on the same page with Mr. Sanders—if you're all right with Asha and her family, then I'm all right with them." He then turned to Mrs. Howard, saying, "Hey, look on the bright side, honey—we're royalty now."

Mrs. Howard calmed down and finally gathered her thoughts. "All right. Even though I'm just now hearing about this, as your mother, I would love it if you could have another wedding here in the City," she said.

"Okay, I'm fine with that. Are you okay with that, Asha?" Jamal asked.

"Yes, I would love to have a wedding here in the City," Asha answered.

"Thank you! Mr. Howard and I will support every creative idea you have for the wedding, and we'll be here with you every step of the way," Mrs. Howard said. Suddenly, she grinned. "Hey, gals, I have an idea," she told Queen Naomi, Lady Iman, and Mrs. Sanders. "We should team up and plan our children's weddings together!"

The ladies were excited and couldn't wait to organize the wedding. "I can bake the wedding cake and make pastries," Mrs. Sanders offered.

"I can decorate!" Lady Iman said.

"I can design the dresses!" Queen Naomi added.

"Great, and I'll find the perfect location!" Mrs. Howard finished.

Moments later, Mrs. Howard got all of the parents together to sit on the couch and chairs in the living room. "Hey guys, I just have to hear the full the story from these kids—young adults, I mean. Tamir, Halima, Jamal, and Asha, I need to know something."

"Yeah, we all do," Mrs. Sanders agreed.

"And what is that?" Asha asked.

"I want to know your story. How did you really meet? How did you fall in love? How did this all happen?" Mrs. Howard asked.

"Oh...well, that's a long story—a really, really long story," Jamal said.

Mrs. Howard smiled and sat on the couch with the rest of the parents, saying, "Well, guess what? I'm all ears."

The End

ABOUT THE AUTHOR

Leonard H. Williams III is also known as Lenny by his peers. He writes, does photography, counsels the youth, and creates documentaries. He plans on making a positive impact on this world by showing children that their differences make them special. Lenny's message to the children: "I'm a proud black man and I'm proud of my heritage. I'm proud of who I am and I love the way God made me. At the same time I care and love the way God has made you all as well. And I care enough to make stories and movies that you can relate to, and identify with because our differences make us all unique and special." "I'm all about embracing our differences not hiding them."

Asha
The Princess of Matana

SPREAD THE MAGIC

-Lenny's Imagination

"NOW LET'S CONVERT THIS WONDERFUL STORY INTO A MOVIE"

Lenny's contact info: sugarraylenny@gmail.com
Kaitlin's contact info: cgkaitlin@gmail.com

lennysimagination.com

Lenny's Imagination

CreateSpace Independent Publishing

Made in the USA
San Bernardino, CA
12 August 2018